The Beginning of a Beautiful Friendship?

Ben looked around the landcar and hefted the little device on the palm of his tanned hand. "So who planted this damn bug under the drive seat?"

"You some kind of screwball or what? Standing here blabbing to yourself."

"Hum?" Ben spun, hand going for the stungun in his new shoulder holster.

"Don't try it, sucker. I don't even have to whip mine out."

A big gunmetal robot, half a head higher than Jolson and broad-shouldered, was walking slowly toward him. He was wearing an impressively bold plaid overcoat and he'd apparently just come out of the Daredevils, Ltd. building.

Holding up his finger, the robot explained, "Built-in kilgun."

"Listen, you dumb ox, what's the big idea threatening me with—"

"Relax, Jolson, relax," said the robot. "Save the hambone stuff for the yokels. I'm wise to youse."

"Who exactly are you?"

"Didn't Sally tell youse about me? I'm Buster." He held out a metal hand. "Shake."

The Exchameleon Book 1

DAREDEVILS, LTD.

RON GOULART

ST. MARTIN'S PRESS/NEW YORK

DAREDEVILS, LTD.

Copyright © 1987 by Ron Goulart

All rights reserved. No part of this book may be used or reproduced in any manner whatsoever without written permission except in the case of brief quotations embodied in critical articles or reviews. For information address St. Martin's Press, 175 Fifth Avenue, New York, N.Y. 10010.

Published by arrangement with the author

Library of Congress Catalog Card Number: 87-50341

ISBN: 0-312-90140-2   Can. ISBN: 0-312-90141-0

Printed in the United States of America

First St. Martin's Press mass market edition/June 1987

10 9 8 7 6 5 4 3 2 1

CHAPTER 1

He was moderately surprised when the young woman came walking in through the wall.

Surprised enough to drop the ceramic snerg he'd been in the process of wrapping for deposit in a shipping carton.

Lunging, Ben Jolson caught the foot-high statuette before it had the chance to smash on the floor of his small warehouse.

"Reflexes still darn good," observed the pretty redhead, brushing the dust from her two-piece sinsatin skirtsuit. "And you're way past forty, Ben."

"Two years isn't, technically, way past, Molly." Jolson eyed the slim intruder, set the rescued snerg on his workbench. "My secsystem is guaranteed to be impervious to wallwalkers."

"Yep, which is why I'm so tickled with this new gadget." When Molly Briggs tapped her midsection, something under the sea-green fabric produced a metallic thunk. "Not only does it efficiently rearrange a person's atoms and allow for easy passing through solid matter, it also futzes up any and all alarm systems. They cost three hundred sixty thousand dollars each, even more if you want silver knobs instead of the standard plaz ones on—"

"Close to a half million trubux so you can walk through my wall instead of the door." Jolson nodded across the carton-filled room toward the sudometal double doors.

"Heck, I'm just simply trying this out on you, Ben." Smiling, she brushed aside wrapping paper and excelsior to perch on his workbench. "We bought six of these for the Briggs Interplanetary Detective Service. Dad and I feel—"

"That reminds me of something I've been meaning to bring up," said the long, lean Jolson. "I know that, when I retired from the Chameleon Corps last year, I did sign a—"

"You better sit down," the red-haired Molly advised. "What I have to say will shock and sadden—"

"How about letting me explain what I've been thinking about first? Then, if you've come to offer me another BIDS assignment—"

"Know what I've been wondering lately, Ben? I'll tell you," she said. "Since you can change and modify your shape, thanks to the lengthy processing and training given you by the Chameleon Corps Division of the Political Espionage Office right here on our planet Barnum, why don't you use that exceptional ability to improve your looks?"

"Improve them?" His left eye narrowed. "How do you suggest I go about—"

"Oh, hey, listen, you're an attractive man," Molly assured him, smiling. "And—did I ever tell you this before? —I had an awful crush on you back when I was a dippy teenager and Dad and you were both crackerjack Chameleon Corps agents, roaming the Barnum System of planets and disguising yoursel—"

"You have told me about the crush on prior occasions, yes," the former Chameleon Corps agent told her. "The first instance took place just before I signed up to be a part-time operative for your half-wit detective agency." He picked up the ceramic snerg and resumed wrapping it.

"All I was getting at, Ben, is that you'd look a heck of a lot handsomer with that grey gone from your temples and that dinky bald spot at the back of your head patched up," continued Molly. "You might, while you were at it, want to do something with those tiny wrinkles under your eyes. Forgive me if, from the vantage point of youth—I'm only twenty-five, after all—I tend to notice—"

"You're twenty-eight."

"Oops—I ought to know better than to lie about my age to an ace investigator like you. What are those ugly things, by the way?" She pointed at the row of pastel-tinted snergs, lined up and waiting to be wrapped, near her resting backside.

"Snergs. Little creatures indigenous to the wretched planets in the Hellquad System. Right now ceramic snergs are considered very collectible out there. I'm teleshipping ten dozen a week. Which is yet another reason I don't have time for taking on detective chores that—"

"Isn't this a coincidence? Because the dreadful, potentially heartrending news I'm bringing you has to do with that selfsame planet complex." She shifted, patting the various flap pockets that fronted her skirt. Locating what she sought, Molly extracted a vial of greyish dust and held it breast high. "Prepare yourself for a shock, Ben."

He glanced at the vial she was holding between thumb and forefinger before finishing wrapping the snerg. "I'm braced."

Agitating the dust in the glaz tube, Molly announced, "This is all that's left of Lou Killdozer."

Nodding, Jolson stuffed the statuette into its carton. "So?"

She wiped at the corner of her eye with the hand that held Killdozer's remains. "Instead of keeping them back, you might be better off letting your true feelings out. I certainly won't think less of you for keening and sobbing over the loss of a comrade in arms, a fellow galactic gumshoe who's—"

"I never met Lou Killdozer." Jolson boosted himself up onto the bench beside her. "Chiefly because all four of the Hellquad planets are several degrees less congenial than a sinkhole. And I usually talked my way out of CC assignments that'd take me out that way. Killdozer was, from all I've heard, a lout and a bully. The whole universe is, more than likely, better off without him."

"Um." Molly lowered her head, watching her fingers smoothing the hem of her short skirt. "That sort of throws a spanner in the works and makes this next part of my pitch sort of rough."

"You were intending to get me to spacejump out to that godforsaken quartet of planets. Four planets that—to quote my longtime chum John Wesley Sand—no matter which one you start from the other three are even worse."

She nodded, long red hair brushing at her shoulders. "Well, I was sort of hoping you'd want to pick up the gauntlet, or whatever they call it, from your fallen fellow op. What I mean is, the code of the private investigator implies—"

"Private investigators maybe. But that's not the code of onetime Chameleon Corps agents who've retired to run their own wholesale ceramics businesses and are growing increasingly uneasy about having let themselves be conned into taking nitwit assignments involving uncomfortable jaunts to the pestholes of the—"

"Sorry you feel that way, because Dad and I both agreed that you were absolutely perfect for this particular assignment," Molly said. "What we must have is a man who can change his shape and appearance."

"You've got five other ex-Chameleons on your payroll," he reminded. "Plus your father."

"Dad's too bogged down with executive duties here on Barnum. And none of our other onetime CC agents have your flair, your ability to improvise, your reliability in—"

"Nope. I've decided I ought to quit BIDS completely," he said. "Nine assignments from you is more than—"

"Guess you haven't as yet heard that the Barnum Supreme Court, in a joint session of both the Humanoid and Android Divisions, has made a unanimous ruling," she said, smiling. "Well, probably not, since it only took place seven minutes ago. Anyhow, the upshot is that—"

"Seven minutes ago? How the hell do you know—"

"Oh, mostly because Dad was somewhat instrumental in getting this pushed through. The point is, if you try to renege on your contract, you're liable to go to Devil's Island #26—that's the sort of run-down one that orbits the second moon of Barafunda. They don't even, as I understand it, have running water in the cells or—"

"Okay, tell me about the damn assignment." Jolson swung down to the warehouse floor.

Molly reached out and patted, absently, one of the snergs on the top of its smooth head. "As you know, Ben," she said, "the Briggs Interplanetary Detective Service has been increasingly successful—"

"Not successful enough to raise my fees."

"That's true. Yet successful enough to be able to branch out across the entire Barnum System and beyond," she went on. "Four and a half months ago we bought a controlling interest in Daredevils, Ltd."

"Lou Killdozer's detective agency out in the Hellquad." He slid the statue out from under her hand and wrapped it in peppermint-stripe paper.

"Despite your low opinion of poor Lou, he and his mother have made Daredevils, Ltd. one of the most prosperous investigative and security agencies out there. They have seven branches thus far, with—"

"His mother, they say, is an even bigger lout and bully than he was. And anybody who'd go into business with his own mother has to—"

"That's no dippier than a grown man who'd rather make snergs than go out into the invigorating environment of the Hellquad—"

"I don't turn out only snergs here."

She glanced around the warehouse. "What are those strange things lurking on that shelf yonder?" she inquired, pointing.

"Owls."

Molly's nose wrinkled. "I guess I only understand representational art."

He said, "Get back to outlining this demeaning job you have in mind for me."

"Since BIDS owns a good portion of Daredevils, Ltd., when they profit, we profit," she said. "Just before poor Lou was killed in the line of duty, he'd had a meeting with a very high official of PlazHartz—they're based on one of the Hellquad planets and are the biggest synthetic-heart producer in the entire universe."

"Farpa."

"Beg pardon?"

"Farpa is the name of the planet that houses Plaz-Hartz."

"Anyway, if Daredevils, Ltd. were to get a contract to handle security for PlazHartz, that would mean a considerable increase in revenues."

"Is that what Killdozer was setting up?"

"We aren't exactly sure," she answered. "Lou, rest his soul, didn't tend to confide in anyone. Not even his mother. So we don't really know for certain what was in the works."

"Can't you just ask his contact at PlazHartz?"

She smoothed her skirt. "Well, we don't want to do that just yet."

Jolson popped a freshly wrapped snerg into its carton. "Ho," he said suddenly, grinning.

"Do you mind my pointing out that when you assume that smug, fatuous expression, those wrinkles I was mentioning earlier really stand out and—"

"They don't," he said, grin still in place, "know that Killdozer is dead."

"As a matter of fact, Ben, they don't," she acknowledged. "He was killed on a seemingly routine divorce case —they still go in for marriage and divorce in the Hellquad —out in the boondocks—"

"The whole planet of Farpa is one vast boondock."

"Lou's unfortunate mother felt—"

"She was once a professional antigrav wrestler."

"The poor woman had him quietly cremated, then spacejumped the remains to us for safekeeping," she said, jiggling the tube of ashes and then setting it down next to the snerg. "It's her notion, heartbroken as she is—"

"Wrestled under the name of Strangler Sally."

"She suggested not letting any of their clients know what had happened just yet," said Molly, frowning at him. "That way we can do things like sending a Killdozer simulacrum to the next meeting with this person at Plaz-Hartz."

He watched her pretty face. "Are you certain Killdozer wasn't knocked off because of something the folks at Plaz-Hartz got him into?"

"Of course I am," she said firmly. "I have Sally Kill-dozer's word on that."

Jolson said, "A bonus."

"Hum?"

"I want fifty thousand trudollars extra to do this one."

"Have that cute little bizcomputer of yours read your contract to you," advised Molly. "You are only entitled to a bonus if and when—"

"Fifty thousand dollars or I don't go."

"But the darn Supreme Court—"

"Devil's Island #26 will look like a spa compared with most of the real estate on the Hellquad planets," he said. "How long a sentence am I likely to—"

"All right, twenty-five thousand."

"Fifty thousand."

"Forty thousand."

He gave an affirmative nod. "I'll leave on the morrow."

"You'll leave before sundown," corrected Molly. "You're booked on a hyperspace flight out of Port/A at six this evening. And you'll be meeting with someone at PlazHartz on the planet Farpa at five tomorrow evening." She lowered herself, gracefully, to the floor. "Don't look so glum and grumpy, Ben. This is a simple, routine assignment."

Jolson picked up the glaz tube and tossed it to her. "That's probably," he said, "what Killdozer thought about the case he was working on."

CHAPTER 2

The skycar dodged around another glaz and neo-metal tower, went fishtailing under a crowded pedramp and then climbed perpendicularly up into the hazy late afternoon. It leveled off high above the city, bounced and shuddered, made a chattering noise deep within its powerful engine and finally commenced flying in the general direction of the spaceport.

"Darn." Molly tugged her skirt down and readjusted the safety gear that held her in the driveseat. "The automatic pilot in this new jalopy isn't functioning as smoothly as it ought to, Ben."

"It flies about the same way you do."

She touched a few more of the dash buttons. "There, we seem to be okay again," she said, glancing out of the cockpit at the territorial capital they were whizzing over. "The reason we paid seven hundred sixty thousand dollars for this particular model skyvehicle is because it allows me to concentrate on things like this briefing while en route to our destination."

"I already know as much about the Hellquad planets as I—"

"The first thing you have to do, Ben, is cooperate." She

twisted, bent and retrieved the visa and ID packet that had fallen to the cabin floor during the unexpected stunting. "Take this stuff and stop refusing to assume—"

"Turning into a catman playboy doesn't bother me." Jolson shifted slightly in the passenger seat. "What I'm perplexed about is having to be one named Pud Humazoo, Jr."

"Well, listen, we aren't the damn Chameleon Corps," she reminded, easing a small vidcaz out of a skirt pocket. "We don't have all that many people to borrow identities from. Puddsie happens to be resting up at a detox spa that orbits one of the Trindad planets off—"

"Puddsie?"

"His nickname."

"I thought Pud was his—"

"No, that's his actual given name." Molly scanned the dash until she spotted the slot she was seeking and then inserted the vidcaz. "The Humazoo family, as you'll learn if you quit grumping and study that dossier, has made untold millions in the music business here in the Barnum System. So I guess, even though you think they have funny names, they happen to be smart enough to earn more in a week than you make all year cranking out snergs and whatall. As Pud's grandfather, Dork Humazoo, has often—"

"Never mind, Molly. I'll assume the identity." He started studying the tri-op photos of Pud Humazoo, Jr.

"While you're getting ready to change into Puddsie, I'll get along with the rest of this briefing." Molly touched a blue button.

". . . another informative Hungerford Brothers Travel-og," boomed the speaker mounted just below the small vidscreen that had come to life at the center of the dash.

The picture, however, consisted of nothing but jagged bits of colored light.

"Greetings, viewers. I'm Ted Hungerford."

"I'm Ned Hungerford. And don't let the fact that we're taping this intro while flat on our backs in Barnum Intensive Care Hospital #26 scare you off."

"That's right, Ned. Our present sorry condition has almost nothing to do with the wonderful and exciting trip we recently made to the Hellquad planets."

"You said it, Ted. Anybody can have a heck of a good time out there, as the Hellquad Tourist Bureau assured us when we evidenced initial reluctance about journeying to an area that's been called—unjustly, we can now assure you—the biggest pesthole in the universe."

"What the dickens." Molly, annoyed, whapped the plaz screen with her fist. "For seven-hundred-sixty-thousand-dollars I want to see more than frizzy lightning bolts."

"I already know more than enough about—"

"C'mon, c'mon." The third smack caused the picture to appear.

The Hungerford Brothers, Ted and Ned, were middle-aged toadmen. At the moment each was in traction in a floating multicare medbed.

". . . there are four planets in the Hellquad, as you might imagine," the toadman with the two broken legs was saying.

"Right you are, Ned," said the other spread-eagled toadman as he attempted to smile around the bandages crisscrossing his pale green face. "Their names are Farpa, Fazenda, Ferridor and Fumaza."

"Despite those rather lackluster names, folks, you'll find the Hellquad planets to be fun-filled places to spend a vacation."

"*If,*" added Ted, "as the Hellquad Tourist Bureau wisely reminds us in their helpful free brochure *How to Survive Your Hellquad Vacation,* you stay in the Safe Zones."

"We can't stress that too much. Never, no matter what your reason, leave the designated safe sectors of each planet. They're all plainly marked so—"

"Perhaps we ought to recount the anecdote about our helpful native guide, Tars Tarkas," suggested Ted. "He was disemboweled near the picturesque Great Festering Swamp Recreational Park because he strayed off the—"

"Sufficient." Reaching out with a paw, Jolson killed the screen.

"You really ought to . . . Golly. You've changed into Pud Humazoo, Jr.," realized Molly. "While I was concentrating on taking in the gist of that informative travelog, as you should've been, you simply transformed yourself."

"Since your father's an ex-Chameleon, you ought to be used to—"

"Dad hasn't done much in that line for years," she said. "And when I was a kid, well, naturally, most if not all of his impersonations were done away from home."

Jolson was now, thanks to the abilities built into him by the long and complex processing he'd undergone many years before while a Chameleon Corps cadet, a convincing facsimile of the ne'er-do-well catman. He was pudgy, in his late twenties, covered with orangish fur and looked to be recovering from a binge of several days' duration.

Molly looked him over, gave an admiring sigh and slid another vidcaz out of a pocket. "Next I want you to see this footage of poor Lou Killdozer," she said. "And you might be able to assimilate more of this important information if you sat up straight."

"That was Port/A we just passed."

"Hmm?"

"Our destination," said Jolson in his burred catman voice. "We flew by it."

"No, we didn't. This brand-new seven-hundred-sixty-thousand-dollar skycar is guaranteed to get us automatically to our . . ." Craning her neck, she stared out the various plaz windows. "We're way out in the doggone suburbs someplace." Angrily, Molly flipped toggles and pressed buttons. "I'll take over and fly us back there myself. We'll study the Killdozer footage a little later."

"I look forward to that." Jolson slouched further in his seat.

CHAPTER 3

The plump birdwoman adjusted her pointed party hat. "I adore kazoo music," she said.

"Really, old girl?" muttered Jolson. He was leaning languidly against the neometal wall of the First-Class Passenger Saloon, taking in the festive scene through half-shut catman eyes.

"That's why I was so very much thrilled, do you know, when I chanced upon the name Fud Humazoo on the passenger list."

"Pud."

"Beg pardon?"

"First name's Pud, dear lady."

"Oh, yes, to be sure. You ought to know. I happen to be Mrs. Martha Novsam," the birdwoman explained. "My husband Jerome and . . . excuse me. Jerome, stop blowing that thing. You're behaving like an idiot."

Near the crowded bar across the room, a gaunt white-feathered birdman in a two-piece bizsuit and a polka-dot party hat had been tooting on a toy trumpet while executing a small tap dance.

"Sorry, love," he called, lowering the horn.

"As I was saying, Mr. Humazoo, I dote on kazoo

music," resumed Mrs. Novsam, still watching her husband. "Your distinguished family manufactures the truest-toned electronic kazoos in the universe."

"I'm flattered, dear lady." Jolson began easing his arm free of her clutching talon.

"I still remember well hearing . . . excuse me again. Jerome, nobody thinks you're at all amusing. Stop that foolish tap dancing."

"Merely demonstrating, love."

"This happens to be a party, not a sales convention," the birdwoman reminded her husband. "As I was saying, I recall hearing Pronzini's Concerto in C Major for Electronic Kazoo and String Orchestra in the famed Barnum Orbiting Philharmonic Hall last seas— Excuse me. Jerome, you're not to sell that young woman any dancing shoes."

"You'd best fly to his side," advised Jolson, moving free of her, dodging one of the festive confetti-spewing servo-bots and nudging his way through a cluster of celebrating fellow passengers to one of the spaceliner's wide viewindows.

He was lounging there, gazing out at the vast dark stillness beyond, when a tall, handsome blonde young woman in a two-piece blue-and-gold unisuit pushed her way to his side. "The captain would like you to join him for a drink," she said with a dazzling smile, "you low abysmal scum."

"How's that, my sweet?"

"Because of my humble position on the crew I can't make a scene in public," she said, continuing to smile falsely. "Yet I have to note that you're behaving true to your loathsome and vile character. Take all sorts of vile familiarities on the last flight and now pretend not to recognize me."

"We've met, then, have we?"

The blonde snorted, straightening up to her full height of near six feet. "I happen to be Midshipwoman Lacey," she informed him, "as you well know, Puddsie."

"Well, how've you been?"

"Your swinish attorneys haven't answered my last two faxgrams," said the young ship's officer in a low voice. "Breach of promise is, granted, much more difficult to prove in cross-species cases. However, the tattoos alone ought to convince any court in the—"

"Tattoos?"

She put her hands on her hips. "Are you even going to pretend you don't remember tattooing low doggerel— well, in fact, they don't even scan well enough to be classed as doggerel—verses on my person? Oh, yes, I realize you were in your cups, as it were, and we'd been snorting zombium and you'd coaxed me to thrust my innocent head into your portable brainstim box with you. Even so, however, you ought to remember some of the rotten—"

"Dear girl, we must certainly talk this over in private later," Jolson assured her. "But no need, really, to spoil the captain's jolly little party."

Midshipwoman Lacey took a deep, angry breath. "You're absolutely right, Puddsie," she said. "You'd best waddle over to the captain's table right now. He's a great fan of kazoo music."

"Many are."

She leaned close to one fuzzy ear. "I'll be in your cabin right after we make our hyperspace jump," she warned. "And you better be prepared to settle things."

Jolson had one hand in a trouser pocket, touching his compact stungun. "I shall, my pet," he promised.

The skycabbie was a husky frogman. As he guided his cab up off the passenger zone of Farpa Spaceport/B2, he inquired, "Bit of a frumus on your liner, buddy?"

Slouched in the backseat, and still in his Pud Humazoo persona, Jolson said, "What makes you ask, old sock?"

"Ambulance went scooting up soon as you docked."

"Yes, well, it seems one of the crew collapsed after the hyperspace jump last evening," he said. "They found the poor lass in the second-class laundry room shortly before landing."

"Funny place to conk out."

"Seemed quite plausible to me."

Shrugging, the driver concentrated on climbing high up into the misty morning. "Where was it you wanted to go, buddy?"

"Capital Plaza Hotel."

"Not as bad a dump as some. Maybe I—urf!" He stiffened suddenly in the driveseat.

"Something amiss, old top?"

The frogman let go of the controls to whap himself several times on the chest. "Just my heart."

"Ought we to set down so you—"

"Naw, it acts up every now and then. I got me an Econ Model-Two PlazHartz heart." After a few more thumps, he relaxed and resumed control of the wavering cab.

Jolson watched his broad back. "Perhaps you'd best land. Allow me to switch to—"

"I'm fit as a kazoo now, bud," the green frogman assured him. "Had this thing near three years now and no real problems. Outside of severe and excruciating pains now and then. Oh, and total blackouts once in a great while."

"What's your notion of a great while, my boy?"

"Not more than once a month, usually."

"Do these spells ever visit you in midflight?"

"Seldom," he said, chuckling. "Not to worry anyways, pal, since this cab's got a swell automatic takeover. Should I suffer one of my seizures, she'll land you safe and sound."

"That's most comforting."

"I almost, you know, didn't buy this brand of replacement heart," confided the cabbie. "See, I was all set to go into the PlazHartz Center in my neighborhood for the implantation, when I hear on the vidnews that Simon Lenz had died. This was, like I said, about three years back."

"Lenz was the fellow who invented the PlazHartz heart, I believe?"

"Yeah, that's the guy," answered the frogman. "So then they announce he'd kicked off at the age of fifty-nine. That didn't seem to speak too well for his product, did it? Heck, though, it turned out Lenz'd died in an accident. His skycruiser crashed out in the sticks somewhere, and you can't blame that on your heart. So I decided to go ahead, and I got to tell you I've never regretted it. Best imitation heart on the market."

"A wise decision, no doubt."

"Sure, because before that, you know, I had pains all the time and lots of blackouts."

Nodding, Jolson turned his attention to the view unfolding beneath the seethru glaz floor of the cab.

They were flying over a safe sector of the capital city of

Farpa's largest territory. The buildings tended to be squat, few higher than five or six stories, and brightly colored. Plaztiles, in basic red, yellow and blue, were the favored roofing material, and Jolson had the impression he was traveling over a vast, gaudy quilt.

"Great tragedy that was," said the frog cabbie.

"Which?"

"When Simon Lenz conked off. I hear it hit his family damn— Urf!" His splayed green fingers flew free of the controls once more. Groaning, he grabbed at his chest and doubled up.

"What say we land, old sport?"

The frogman groaned once before slumping forward and passing out.

The skycab started zigzagging down through the misty sky.

"Damn." Jolson unfastened his safety harness as swiftly as he could with his furry paws.

"Warning," squawked the voxbox on the dented dash. "Dire warning, in fact. You are flying free of a Safe Zone."

"I can see that." Jolson was aware the city was changing beneath his feet.

Bright colors were giving away to grey, complete buildings were being replaced by tottering ruins.

Scrambling over its back, he dropped into the passenger seat next to the stricken driver.

"Warning, warning. Unless you pull up at once, you'll crash smack-dab into Basher Park. Unsafe! Unsafe! Let me go even further and state it's a veritable hellhole, swarming with—"

"Hush." Jolson tried to take control of the skycab around the lax body of the frog cabbie.

"Hold on to your hats!" warned the dash.

Before Jolson could do much of anything, the skycab slammed down into a muddy clearing amidst a grove of dark, gnarled trees.

CHAPTER 4

Jolson was standing ankle deep in muck, paws on hips, surveying the vicinity. To his immediate left was sprawled the downed skycab, its nose burrowed deep in mud and prickly weeds. Inside the cabin were the unconscious frogman cabbie and the completely destroyed communications system.

To his right stretched a grove of stunted, ungainly trees. A few bedraggled luminous squirrels were dozing in the twisted branches. Bolted to the splotched grey trunk of a near tree was an engraved neometal sign reading WELCOME TO BASHER PARK! PROCEED AT YOUR OWN RISK! MAY BE FATAL AFTER NIGHTFALL! SCREW YOUSE! The last phrase had been artistically added by hand in glopaint.

Another sign, posted on a further tree, announced PUBLIC PHONE THIS WAY SCREW YOUSE!

Nodding to himself, Jolson set out in pursuit of the pixphone. His snergskin playboy shoes made slurping sounds as he walked across the muck.

A yellowish, acrid mist was drifting through the dark woods. Up in the gnarled branches the squirrels began to cough.

From a distance noise commenced. Some sort of vastly amplified, raucous, brassy music, great crashing and thumping sounds, a few brief screams of pain.

The first pixphone kiosk he came to lay on its side in a patch of purplish moss. Most of the screen looked to have been chomped away by something with large, powerful dentures.

He scratched his furry catman head, remarking, "This caper is not getting off to a sparkling start."

He trudged on.

Three frail grey-haired human ladies came sprinting over a rise. They were shrieking, clutching their purses to their narrow chests. They were running straight toward Jolson.

Leaping in among the gloomy trees, he waited until they'd dashed by before returning to the muddy pathway.

The advent of two more running, screaming ladies caused him to hop aside yet again.

Around the next bend were the remains of a neowood bench. Seated on its rickety skeleton, perusing a tabloid consisting entirely of multicolored comics, was a plump dogman in a three-piece yellow bizsuit.

"Care to wager?" he inquired, lowering his funnies.

"On what, old cork?"

"The outcome of the minimarathon," replied the dogman, panting some. "Little-old-lady victims versus heartless park muggers. An annual event in Basher."

"Not my kind of gambling." He halted. "What I am interested in, though, is a public phone in working order."

The dogman shook his head. "Hasn't been one of those in Basher Park since . . . let's see, now . . ." Holding up a gloved paw, he started ticking off fingers. "Must be five years at least."

"Really, now? That puts me in a bit of a bind, what with a crashed skycab and—"

"Yowie!" The comic tab rose into the air, bright-colored pages flapping like wings, and the dogman executed an impressive backward somersault over the remnants of the bench. "Run for it, friend." He followed his own advice, trotting briskly off into the surrounding woods.

Turning, Jolson confronted what it was that had prompted the dogman's departure.

"Can you lads suggest where I might find a functioning pixphone?" he asked the six immense gorillamen who loomed on his horizon.

Each was a muddy brown color, each was clad in a two-piece checkered cazsuit and each wore a plaz derby tilted at a rakish angle on his large, shaggy head.

"Do a scramola," suggested the next-to-largest gorilla-man.

"Wait now, Ernie," said another. "We come into the park for a workout. Tearing this sissy limb from limb, why, that'd be darn good exercise."

"Naw, Dow," said Ernie, removing his seethru derby to buff its crown on his checkered elbow. "Look it up. That sort of exercise burns hardly any calories."

"But suppose," put forth another gorilla, "after we rip him to pieces, we yank out his innards and jump rope with them?"

"Sure," said Dow, nodding, "that'd be darn good aerobic exercise."

"His innards won't last more than a few minutes," Ernie pointed out as he replaced his hat. "Remember the alderman last month?"

"Yeah, but he was a little dinky birdman. This is a big bulky catman."

"What've we got to lose?" said the largest check-suited gorillaman. "We're bound to have some fun rending this guy asunder and gutting him. If it turns out we don't elevate our pulse rate all that much, what the hey? Life isn't all diet and exercise, you know."

Jolson cleared his throat. "Gents, I don't mind all this talk of violence," he said, reaching casually under his jacket. "What does annoy me, though, are these slurs on my manhood. I'll have you know I'm an intergalactic playboy, rated as— Oof!"

A seventh gorilla had grabbed him from behind, pinning his arms to his sides. "He was going for a weapon."

"That tips the scales, far as I'm concerned," said Dow.

"Chaps, it's merely a stungun," explained Jolson amiably. "Small one at that."

"What say we rip off one of his arms anyway? If that doesn't cheer us up, we can quit."

"Naw, that's too sissified. Go for the whole—"

"Hey, you walleyed galoots! What do you think you're up to?"

"Um . . ."

"Um . . ."

Six of them shuffled their big feet, tipped their derbies, looked uneasy.

A big, broad woman came striding up. "What about you, Milt?"

The gorilla who was gripping Jolson said, "Um." He let go, took two uncertain steps back and lifted his hat to her.

She was clad in a billowing two-piece suitdress of a pattern that resembled a field of exploding flowers. Her face was wide and weather-worn, her nose flattened, her frizzy hair an improbable shade of blond. "That's better," she announced in her gravelly voice. "Now suppose you clear off of my old buddy, Pud."

Dow snickered. "Pud? What kind of—"

"Suppose you bozos take a hike," she suggested. "Damn soon."

"Yes, ma'am."

"Yes, ma'am."

"Nice seeing you again, Sally."

"See you around."

"Give our best to Lou."

They retreated, jogging rapidly off and away.

The woman slapped Jolson on the back. "You can't let any of these lop-eared bastards bully you," she told him. "I happen to be Sally Killdozer and I arranged for this little meeting to take place here. How's that for a pleasant surprise?"

"It's a surprise, anyway," he said.

CHAPTER 5

Settling her substantial backside on an uprooted log, Sally Killdozer lit a fat kelp cigar. "What I'm getting at, kiddo, is security," she told Jolson, exhaling plumes of smoke.

Paws in pockets, Jolson was leaning against the base of a lopsided neobronze statue that depicted a toadman general mounted on a rearing grout. "Basher Park doesn't strike me as the most secure spot on the face of—"

"Trust me, it's safer than you waltzing right into the Daredevils, Ltd. offices in the heart of town got up as a hung-over kazoo scion," the lady detective told him. "See, Benny, I'm worried about—"

"Don't use my real name, or a nitwit variation," he warned, brushing at his whiskers.

"Holy Hannah, do you think I'm an apple-knocker? I checked this whole area out for bugs and soundguns and all that other snooping hardware before I ever had the skycab dump you here."

"Even so," he said. "Right now I'm nobody but Pud Humazoo, Jr. And the reason I adopted this identity in the first place, Sally, was as a security measure. That way I can visit any place I—"

"Theoretically, sure." She took a deep drag on the stogie. "Here's what I'm trying to get across, lover. We maybe got us an extra problem or two."

"Such as?"

"For one thing, somebody tried to break into our offices early this morning."

"Don't you have a secsystem that—"

"Yeah, we got all that crap. And soon as we sold out to Briggs his flighty daughter sent us out an additional setup. The new one's supposed to administer a minor shock to any break-in artist who so much as puts a pinkie to a door or window. Cost three hundred sixty thousand dollars, she told me."

"Did you catch anybody?"

Smoke swirled as Sally shook her head. "Not so it'd do us any good," she said. "This guy had a bum ticker—one of those no-frills PlazHartz jobbers—and the minor shock did him in. I found the bozo lying in state in the downstairs foyer when I come in this A.M."

"You identify him?"

"Not yet. He was a birdman cyborg. Metal hands and glaz eyes, so no prints to go by. No ID packet on him, no labels or ultramarx in his duds." Sally shrugged. "On top of which, the electrical shock fried his feathers pretty good and he isn't all that presentable."

"You sure this has something to do with the case I'm here to work on?"

"Got no proof, honey, no. Still, though, I got me a strong hunch it all ties in."

"What exactly was your son working on?"

Removing the cigar from between her lips, Sally knuckled the corner of an eye. "Gee, look at me, getting all puddly over Lou," she said, sniffling. "He was one hell of a shamus, and I don't think you, or anybody, can come close to impersonating him."

"The case?"

"Right, back to business." She sniffled a few more times before chomping again on the cigar. "Actually, honey, every blessed thing I knew I told Molly Briggs. Lou always played his cases close to the vest, never made any notes or reports until he'd tied it all up."

"What about his death?" asked Jolson. "Molly didn't have any details on that. Who was respons—"

"Gosh, you don't give a grieving mom much of a break." She sighed out smoke. "Listen, I don't know who did Lou in or why. He was supposed to be trailing a wayward spouse. Wayward toadman with considerable dough and four wives. Three of them suspected the old gink was fooling around and came to Daredevils, Ltd."

"How was he killed?"

Sally threw the stogie into the mud. "My guess is that somebody monkeyed with his skycar."

"Guess?"

"The report I got came from the territorial cops out near the Great Festering Swamp Recreational Park," explained Lou Killdozer's mother. "Apparently an off-duty forest ranger saw Lou's skycar crash into one of those big damn pools of quicksand and sink. Made one hell of a slurp, according to this eyewitness. There isn't any way you can fish anything out of a bog like that. So we really won't ever—"

"Hold it, now." He came closer to her. "Molly showed me Lou's ashes. How'd you manage to—"

"Aw, that was simply a symbolic gesture," explained Sally, pointing a booted foot at her cigar butt. "I just filled a bottle with ashes from my smokes. Whenever you can, toss in a visual aid. Helps make your—"

"So you faked the evidence," said Jolson, "and Molly and her dad were too dim-witted even to analyze the ashes."

"Lou's dead," Sally said, "that's for sure."

"That you can't even prove."

She fisted her bosom. "I know."

Jolson turned away from her. "Is the appointment still on for this afternoon with the PlazHartz client?"

"You meet him at his home at five. Or rather Lou does," she said. "Are you sure you can turn into a reasonable enough—"

"Does anybody else know Lou's no longer around?" he asked, facing her again.

"Nobody, not a damn soul. I got to tell you, that's taken some doing," she said. "My only boy defunct and me yearning to start mourning and lamenting, to deck myself out in black. Couple mornings I caught myself on the brink of buying wreaths to hang on the damn doors. But I managed to keep my natural maternal feelings bottled up."

"The PlazHartz account could bring in several million trubux a year."

Sally shot to her feet. "Are you implying, lover, that I put dough before sentiment?"

"Yep."

She eyed him for several silent seconds. "Well, I guess maybe you're right," she admitted finally. "If we can keep them thinking Lou is still alive, for a while anyway, it could mean a big fee for all concerned." Sally tugged a fresh cigar from her dress pocket. "Now we better beat it.

Come to the office at four—as Lou—and I'll arrange your transport to the client's digs."

"It's okay to appear there as Lou?"

"Sure, since we want everybody to think he's still above the sod." She patted him on the back. "You're a heartless bastard, but I think maybe I'm going to like you."

Jolson said nothing.

"Dang," remarked the bearded bellhop when he dropped the suitcase for the second time. "That is one heavy mother." Rather than pick it up immediately, he slumped down on the yellow stairway step beside it. "This goshdarn climb ain't doing my delicate lungs no good at all."

"Three stories isn't much of an ascent." Jolson moved a paw, caught the suitcase handle. "I'll heft it. Now let's continue—"

"Just a dang minute, mister. Don't you go touching that," warned the wheezing bellhop as he slapped a knobby hand over Jolson's furry fingers. "You carry your luggage and you'll be wiping out near to sixteen years of gradual progress in the sphere of labor negotiations hereabouts."

"How so?"

"Ain't you never heard of the prolonged and far from harmonious strikes brought against all the hotels in these parts? Really was something." He rose to his feet, swaying and quivering slightly, and got hold of the piece of luggage. "You might help out to the extent of aiding me in getting her off the dang step, mister."

Jolson obliged. "If the elevators were functioning, all this wouldn't be—"

"Hellsfire, the goshdarn things work just fine," he said.

"Reason we can't use them right now is because both the operators is pie-faced drunk in the cantina down the block." Staggering some with the suitcase, he resumed climbing toward Jolson's fifth-floor suite. "See, it's all part of the Hire a Human movement."

"Hire them instead of androids and robots?"

"Exactly, you're catching on right good." He paused on the fourth-floor landing to gasp. "Getting a decent job was fierce until we got them to agree to quotas."

"Nobody's watching just now. Let me carry that so we can make better—"

"Nosir." The bellhop clutched the groutskin bag to his small chest and started onward. "I mean to say, there are beliefs you fight and die for. If I didn't perform better than a goldang andy, then I'd— Whoops."

The suitcase left him again, dropped on a step and started bouncing back down the way they'd climbed.

Jolson spun, caught it and kept it. "I'll look after this from here on up."

"But the whole battle for—"

"Have you ever tumbled down three or four flights of stairs?"

"Can't say as I have, but what—"

"Then don't add it to your experiences." Jolson began to go up, two steps at a time.

He found the first one under the floating Lucite coffee table in his living room.

Using the hand-sized detector he'd taken out of his suitcase, Jolson had started hunting as soon as the bearded bellhop caught his breath and left the room.

The microbug was stuck to one of the table legs. Detaching the eavesdropping gadget, he carried it over to a tinted viewindow. By adjusting his eyes, he could read the minute words inscribed on the spec-sized disc: *Ace Discount Spy Equipment Warehouse. Why Pay More?*

He crouched beside the room's dispozhole, flicked the bugging device off his furry fingertip and into oblivion.

This bug was the one planted by the Capital Plaza Hotel itself. His research on Barnum had told him that the whole chain used this particular brand.

Jolson resumed searching.

Outside, the day was clouding over, greying the bold reds, yellows and blues of the surrounding rooftops.

The second listening device was larger, more sophisticated. The detector sniffed it out under the lid of the hamper in the bath cubicle.

Manufactured in the Barnum System, it was of a type not widely in use out here in the Hellquads.

Jolson tossed it, caught it on his furry palm, tossed it, caught it. After dismantling the thing, he popped it into his suitcase and wrapped it in a plaid sock.

Sixteen minutes later, satisfied there was no more spying equipment in his suite, Jolson blanked all the windows. He settled down in a tin slingchair and returned to his true self. Or almost his true self. He'd decided to cover up that small bald spot Molly Briggs had pointed out.

"The hotel planted the first bug," he said to himself, drumming his fingertips on his knee. "But who's responsible for the other one?"

Only Sally Killdozer and Molly knew he was going to be registered here at the Plaza as Pud Humazoo, Jr.

"Or so you think," he reminded himself.

Could well be that both ladies had confided in others. Might even be that the folks who'd tried to break into Daredevils, Ltd. knew of his arrival.

"Nope, that's unlikely."

Stretching up out of the chair, he began pacing the room.

"And what about Lou Killdozer's demise? Who arranged it?"

Or had it happened at all?

"I really have to get into the ceramics business full-time."

From out of the suitcase he fetched the vidcaz Molly had given him. It contained about forty minutes of vid talk-show interviews with Lou.

Somewhat reluctantly, Jolson stuck the caz into the living-room vidviewer and sat down to study again the man he was about to become.

CHAPTER 6

Jolson grabbed two of the pickpocket's four wrists. "You aren't too deft, meatball," he remarked, tossing the green man against a nearby blue brix wall.

"Hey, sorry, Lou, I didn't recognize you from behind."

Grinning, Jolson relit his kelp stogie. "We all make mistakes," he said in his new raspy voice. "And anybody can make one with Lou Killdozer. But pull number two, pal, and you'll be pushing up daisies. You get me?"

"Sure, Lou, sure." The verdant pickpocket nodded. "Like I say, I didn't tumble right off it was you. I don't know, you wasn't walking with your usual—how shall I put it?—swagger."

"Keep your nose clean, kiddo." Puffing on his cigar, Jolson continued along the early-afternoon sidewalk, up-grading his swagger.

This was a Safe Sector, its wide streets treelined and moderately thronged with pedestrian traffic.

Jolson, who was now a fairly accurate duplicate of the swarthy, broad-shouldered Lou Killdozer, walked briskly along the yellow sidewalk. He passed a liquor store that was having a Special Sale on Earth Wines, a multisex barbershop, a gourmet vegetarian restaurant and a garden-furniture store that was offering Incredible Prices on Ceramic Snergs. He slowed, hunched slightly and gave the array of snergs behind the tinted window the once-over.

"Damn," he muttered. "Cheesy imitations of my snergs, and selling for six more trubux apiece."

"Hey, Lou, you going swish on us?"

He turned, teeth gripping the cigar tightly. "Who the hell's the wise guy who—"

"Relax, fella, I was just only kidding," said the sparkling white street-cleaning robot who was eying him from the lavender gutter. "I mean, you ain't usually to be found eyeballing objects of art."

"Geez, these dornicks aren't art."

The robot's white ball of a head had *Dept. Sanit.* stenciled in red across the forehead. It nodded in a sly come-on-over way. "I was looking all over for you. Where you been?"

"Around, pal." Jolson approached him, remembering to swagger.

"New suit, ain't it, Lou?"

"Yeah, like it?"

The robot said, "Sure, that shade of yellow becomes you, and I like them checks. But let me level with you, I'd regulate the sox some."

"You figure they're blinking too brightly?"

"A little," said the streetcleaner. "I mean, far be it from me to give dress tips to a fashion plate such as yourself, but . . . a word to the wise. The necktie is gorgeous, though."

"I had a moment when I thought maybe a few less migrating grackles flying across it would be more tasteful, but then I decided to go with the whole damn flock."

"A wise choice." The robot's round head tilted, his

voice dimmed. "I got your dough from Hal the Bookie. Want it now?"

"Which bet is this?" he asked out of the side of his mouth.

"The grout race, what else?"

"What indeed. Sure, hand it over."

"Pretend you're dropping something in my garbage bin," instructed the robot. "Reach in and the moolah'll land in your mitt."

"Same as always," guessed Jolson. "You don't have to tell me every time."

"Some of our clients ain't so bright as you." A panel on the mechanism's white front popped wide open.

Jolson thrust in a hand and, after encountering part of a muskmelon and a grout cheese sandwich, had a bundle of cash deposited in his palm. "Much obliged. How's Hal doing?"

"Hell of a lot better since he got his PlazHartz heart. I'll tell him you was asking." The voice dropped even lower. "Want to lay a bet on the snerg fights?"

"Skip it. I'm trying to taper off." Giving the robot a lazy salute, he sauntered off toward the Daredevils, Ltd. office building.

On the next corner a windup mechanical preacher was passing out leaflets. "Repent," he advised Jolson. "Repent before it is too late."

"I intend to," Jolson assured the machine, "shortly."

Jolson came bounding across the threshold of the big reception room. He tipped off his plaz fedora, sent it flying toward the distant hatrack. "In for two," he said, shifting his smoldering cigar to the other side of his wide mouth.

There was a very pretty blue-haired young woman in a

one-piece sinsilk glosuit seated at the floating rubberoid desk. She smiled, a bit tentatively, at him.

"Hiya, angel," Jolson said, striding over to her. He parked his buttocks on her desk edge, leaned, removed his stogie and kissed her on the lips. "How's tricks, Fritzi?"

Quite close to his battered right ear the receptionist said, "I was terribly worried about you, Lou. What I mean is, I haven't seen you for just days and days."

"Hell, that's the way an op's life gets sometimes, sweetheart."

She pressed her fingertips to her breast. "What I was worried about, Lou, is I thought they'd killed you."

Jolson puffed on his cigar. "Who specifically?"

"You know who I mean."

"You aren't talking about . . . ?"

"Yes, yes." She nodded vigorously. "My husbands. They suspect."

"All of them, huh?"

"Well, no, actually Jack is too dim to have tumbled that you and I have been fooling around," said Fritzi. "And Ray may know but he doesn't really much care. The other three, though, have been making all sorts of nasty threats."

He chuckled. "Aw, they haven't got any nerve. No use getting the jitters over those meatballs."

"They went out and bought a gun."

"A gun each?"

"No, one awfully big gun that I think takes about three or four husky men to operate." She put her hand on his arm, squeezing some. "Promise me you'll be careful. Real extra careful."

"I always am, angel cake."

"Maybe, you know, we ought not to see each other till this blows over."

"That's a smart notion, kiddo." Kissing her on the cheek, he left her desk to head for Killdozer's office.

He was about halfway there when Sally emerged from her office, spotted him and exclaimed, "My golly, Lou, you're alive!"

Jolson laughed. "So they tell me, Ma." He hurried over to the hefty woman, urged her back into her office. "Takes more than a trio of irate spouses to knock Lou Killdozer off."

"Lou, I went and asked that skinny Molly Briggs to fix up a ringer to—"

"Shut your yap, Ma." He shut the door with his brogan, guided her to her swivel chair and settled her, none too gently, into it. "It's me."

"I know it's you, Lou." Snatching up a folder from the desktop, Sally began fanning her pale face and gasping in air. "Gosh, those walleyed bastards told me you got sucked up by quicksand out in the Great Festering—"

"I'm Jolson," he said quietly.

She set the folder down. "You're who?"

"Jolson," he mouthed.

"What the hell's the big idea of coming in here and shocking a poor grieving mother out of—"

"That's what I'm supposed to be doing." He took a step back from her, flicking cigar ashes on the thick thermorug. "You made the deal, remember?"

"I did, yeah, you're right." She still didn't seem to have her breathing under control. "But, hot damn, you look and act so much like poor darling Lou that—"

"I *am* Lou." Jolson pointed the cigar at her. "And you can't keep futzing up like you just did, not anymore.

Far as you're concerned I'm your own dear son. Got that, Ma?"

She scowled up at him, bit at the inside of her cheek. "Okay, but there's no need to be so mean and nasty to—"

"To Strangler Sally," he cut in. "Now cease the deep-mourning act and fill me in on the client I have to go visit."

"You're being even rottener than Lou ever was."

"That's because I don't want to end up like he did."

CHAPTER 7

He made another slow circuit of the low sea-blue landcar. Then, slipping the small detector back into a side pocket of his yellow bizsuit, Jolson glanced around the small Daredevils, Ltd. parking lot.

There was a high one-way glaz wall all around it and a glaz dome roof. There was an entrance from the ground floor of the offices and the only way to get to the street was by driving through a voxprint gate.

"So who planted this damn bug under the driveseat?" He hefted the little device on the palm of his tanned hand.

It was the same brand as the one he'd rooted out in his bathroom at the hotel.

"Are they interested in me or in Lou Killdozer? Or in the both of us?"

"You some kind of screwball or what? Standing here blabbing to yourself."

"Hmm?" He spun, hand going for the stungun in his new shoulder holster.

"Don't try it, sucker. I don't even have to whip mine out."

A big gunmetal robot, half a head higher than Jolson and broad-shouldered, was walking slowly toward him.

He was wearing an impressively bold plaid overcoat and he'd apparently just come out of the Daredevils, Ltd. building.

Holding up his forefinger, he explained, "Built-in kilgun."

"Listen, you dumb ox, what's the big idea threatening me with—"

"Relax, Jolson, relax," said the robot. "Save the hambone stuff for the yokels. I'm wise to youse."

"Who exactly are you?"

"Didn't Sally tell youse about me? I'm Buster." He held out a metal hand. "Shake."

"Just as well not."

"Think I got a joybuzzer built in?"

Jolson said, "You work for the agency?"

"Sure, you got it. I was Lou's bodyguard and driver."

"Where were you when he got himself—"

"Don't think I ain't razzed myself over that, pal," said Buster. "The boss tells me he wants a little privacy that particular day. I figures he's aiming to rassle in the sack with one of his broads. I let him go off on his own, and that turns out to be a sap move."

Jerking a thumb in the direction of the landcar, Jolson asked, "Who else uses this one?"

"Nobody. It was Lou's exclusive."

"How about this?"

"A bug. So?"

"Tell me who planted it in the car."

Buster said, "That's the kind Lou liked to use. It's probably just a leftover from—"

"Nope. This one was concealed under the driveseat."

The robot's head made a faint creaking noise when he

shook it. "Beats the hell out of me, pal," he admitted. "I never let nobody near this heap. Lou didn't neither."

"When's the last time you drove the car?"

"Couple days before the boss croaked."

"It's been sitting here since?"

"Sure." Buster took a few lurching steps closer. "This got something to do with Lou's getting bumped off?"

"Might." Jolson added the dismantled bug to his pocket.

The car swirled around another corner. A flung neo-metal crutch, abandoned by a venerable toadman who'd gone diving for the safety of the blue sidewalk, thunked on the hood and spun away.

"Shake a leg, granpappy," advised Buster.

"What say," suggested Jolson, "we modify our pace."

"Listen, Jolson, youse is supposed to be Lou—although if youse ask me youse is too much of a pansy to bring it off—and Lou and me is known for roaring around this burg."

"One deceased Lou is enough. Slow down."

"Youse is the boss." Slowing the vehicle, Buster made a few complaining noises deep inside his metal chest. "Wasn't bad enough youse dragged Sally out to give me the once-over before you even allow me to drive you to see this gink. Naw, now youse got to insist we drive around like a couple of nancys."

"This Wally O'Brine I'm calling on," said Jolson. "What do you know about him?"

"He pulls down four hundred sixty thousand trubux per annum from the PlazHartz outfit," said the robot. "I never myself cared for gatormen of his particular shade of green, but some—"

"How many times did you drive Lou out to O'Brine's place in Farmland #3?"

Holding up two metallic fingers, Buster answered, "Deuce."

"Did Lou meet him anywhere else? At PlazHartz or—"

"Naw. The boss was just getting started on the case when he kicked off."

"Any idea what he was consulting the agency about?"

"O'Brine's high up in the PlazHartz outfit. My guess'd be they was thinking of having us take over plant security and employee screening. That's a specialty of—"

"What do you know for certain, Buster?"

"Not a whole hell of a lot," the robot replied. "See, me and Lou never much talked about business. Mostly we gabbed about dames or sports. Grout racing, botboxing and—"

"Did you go in with Lou when he called on the client?"

"Waited in the jalopy. Some people don't go for having a robot around listening in."

"So you never saw O'Brine?"

"Not even once."

"Anything unusual happen on either visit?"

"Don't think so, pal. I hung around the car, keeping my eyes open. O'Brine's got the place fortified like a bank, and it could be the guy's scared about something. Or he's got some stuff stashed around there he don't want nobody grabbing."

"Details?"

"I'm only guessing."

They'd left the city and were roaring along a broad highway that cut through rolling fields of yellow grain.

"Lou never told you what O'Brine wanted?"

"Naw, he was real closemouthed."

"So I keep hearing," said Jolson.

Three rooms away, in a sunlit dining pavilion, three blonde young human women laughed and chatted around a floating plexitable. Their voices drifted through open doorways and along pale corridors, reaching Jolson in the huge glaz-walled den as faint murmurs.

Out on the broad slanting lawn two chrome-plated guardogs sat patiently in anticipation of any intruders who managed to get through the forcedome and then over the ten-foot-high brix wall topped with stunstripz.

There was a warm haze in the late-afternoon air, blurring the sharp green of the grass and the silvery glare of the sharp-toothed metallic hounds.

"You ought not to do these things to me, Killdozer. Ought not at all." A fat gatorman came hurrying in, wearing gloshorts and a billowing terrirobe.

"Keep your skivvies on, O'Brine." Jolson puffed on his cigar and kept his shoes resting atop the sudomarble coffee table.

"You haven't contacted me for days. I wasn't even sure you'd show up today," complained the green client. "I'm living in terror, in mortal dread and terror."

Nodding in the direction of the chittering girls, Jolson asked, "Don't your broads cheer you up any?"

"We went into this before." O'Brine sat on the edge of an inflated rubberoid sofa and glowered. "There is no need, absolutely no need at all, to make sarcastic remarks about my style of—"

"You hire Lou Killdozer and you're stuck with his personality," Jolson told the nervous green gatorman.

"Maybe what you need is some kind of pussyfooting dick who—"

"No, no, I want you," insisted O'Brine apologetically. "But, Killdozer, my life's in danger and you haven't even—"

"Been following up leads," Jolson told him. "See, detective work is mostly patient—"

"Three murders in a little over a month would make anyone jumpy and uneasy." His jaws opened wide and then shut with an anxious chomp. "I mean to say, three high-placed executives at PlazHartz slaughtered by a phantom and—"

"Your company's still keeping all this hushed up." This was a guess. Jolson had been sleepbriefed on the Plaz-Hartz organization back on Barnum, and since arriving on Farpa he'd looked up the company on the refchannel of his hotel-suite vidwall. Nowhere had he encountered mention of any recent killings.

"Do you think they want a panic? Do you think they want the stock to plummet?" Yanking a plyochief from a pocket of his robe, he dabbed at his warty snout.

"If the cops could nose around, then—"

"Certain important police officials are discreetly investigating, as I told you on your last visit." He frowned. "You'll also recall I told you to make notes. Trusting to an organic brain is foolhardy as well as—"

"The old Lou Killdozer grey matter is still ticking along okay." Jolson took a puff of his fat cigar.

"Now about the list."

"The list," Jolson echoed.

"I drew it up, as you requested, but you never contacted me about—"

"Here I am, kiddo. Hand it over." He extended his left hand, palm up.

O'Brine located a folded sheet of blue faxpaper in another pocket. After carefully unfolding it, he passed it to the detective. His big green hand was shaking. "There's no way of telling, no way at all, when my turn will come," he said. "I could well be next."

"Nobody's going to bump you off with Daredevils, Ltd. on the job." He scanned the list of names.

There were thirteen, men and women. The top three had been crossed out with red ink.

O'Brine wiped at his snout again. "Something has come up, something new that I'd better tell you."

"Go ahead," Jolson invited, dropping the list to the table.

"Mary Jane Mougin saw something," said the gatorman. "She hasn't told anyone except myself—no police and no one at Plaz."

Jolson casually took a look down at the list. There was no one named Mougin. "Which of these bozos was she shacking up with?"

O'Brine's many teeth showed in an angry grimace. "The relationship Mary Jane had with poor Leo Thackamason, I'll have you know, was a beautiful—"

"Thackamason. The second exec to bite the dust. Who'd this babe see?"

"Look here, Killdozer, if you interview Miss Mougin you'll have to behave in a much more respectful—"

"Spill," he urged. "Why should I waste time gabbing with this particular skirt at all?"

"She . . . she was at poor Leo's when . . . when it happened. The police . . . no one knows that. Mary Jane saw . . . got a glimpse actually of the killer."

"She's just now getting around to mentioning the fact?"

"Leo's death was, I mean to say, a great blow to her and she's only coming out of it now. After all, he was only killed three weeks ago," said O'Brine. "Besides, she was afraid—and who wouldn't be?"

Jolson said, "All the people on your list work at Plaz-Hartz."

"Of course, yes. I told you that last time, and had you had the sense to make notes or use a voxcorder, you wouldn't be going over this ground again now," the client said. "What they have in common is that they are—or were—employees of Plaz."

"But what else?"

The gatorman looked away, chomping on air a few times. "Nothing."

"C'mon. PlazHartz has forty-six hundred people working in its main complex in this territory." He grabbed up the list and waved it a few times. "How come there aren't forty-six hundred names on this list?"

"These thirteen are, I sincerely believe, in more danger than any of the others."

Jolson slowly refolded the list, tapped it a few times on his broad, flattened nose. "You're not leveling with me," he accused. "That makes it tougher to save your butt."

"What you have to do is keep me from being killed," reminded the client. "I already put in the extra security devices you suggested. What you have to do is dig further into the killings, get a lead to the killer and stop—"

"The long damn way around." He slid the list into the breast pocket of his yellow suit. "Simon Lenz died, too. Earlier than any of these folks. Written off as an accident at the time, but I wonder—"

"We had, none of us, anything to do with Simon's death. No matter what that insane girl has said."

"You talking about Jennifer Lenz? The girl they dumped in a funny farm?"

"The unfortunate young woman was, I mean to say, morbidly attached to her late father," said the green Plaz-Hartz executive. "His entirely accidental passing pushed Jennifer over the edge. Sad, but humans can be fragile that way." He turned, glanced down the corridors at the distant girls.

"You could turn out to be sort of fragile yourself, Jocko," said Jolson, chomping on his cigar.

CHAPTER 8

The blonde woman was in her late thirties and pretty, but there was a bit too much of her. She slightly overflowed the chrome armchair and her hand nearly hid the window viewselector she was clutching. "This isn't my home, Mr. Killdozer," she was explaining to Jolson. "Fact of the matter, it gives me the heebie-jee-bies. Sixteen stories underground—it's like being buried and in your grave. Giving a condocomplex a fancy name like Downside Estates and charging incredible prices doesn't change that. I'm simply, you understand, house-sitting for a friend of mine who's off vacationing in a parallel universe. Her name is Florabelle Beesecker, which has always struck me as an—"

"What say, sister," interrupted Jolson in his raspy Killdozer voice, "we cut the crap and get down to business."

Mary Jane Mougin looked toward the wide window beside her. The view was of a placid jungle lagoon. "I'm not in the mood for foliage," she said, poking a control button on the viewselector.

The window shimmered, went black. A vast snow-covered plain with a harsh wind blowing across it appeared.

"Tell me about your boyfriend's murder." He puffed on his foul-smelling cigar.

"Leo and I weren't exactly romantically linked," said Mary Jane, her eyes on the swirling snow. "It was more a deep friendship sort of thing."

"You saw something the day he was killed."

"Do you like snow?"

"Can take it or leave it alone. Tell me about—"

"It seems to be giving me snerg bumps." She shuddered, jiggling in the shiny chair. "Let's try the tropics." A pudgy forefinger jabbed a button.

The view changed to one of a peaceful green island in a calm sea of blue.

"Were you in Thackamason's house in Farmland #1 when—"

"No, not exactly." She shook her head. "Thank goodness I wasn't or I might have been killed as well. I most certainly would have suffered Leo's fate."

"What was that?"

"He's dead. You know that, don't you?"

"But it's been hushed up, angel. I haven't gotten a look at any report on it," Jolson explained. "So I'd like to know how he was done in."

She shivered again. "You aren't a pleasant man," Mary Jane said. "I really had hoped talking to you would help me relax and lift the burden of—"

"For that you need a priest or a noodle doctor, sister."

She returned her gaze to the view. A tiny sailboat was now gliding along the blue horizon. "He was shot with a kilgun. It . . . it made an awful ugly hole right through his chest. Leo was a very handsome man for his age and he had a very attractive chest, muscular and tan. They made an awful hole—"

"They? Was there more than one who—"

"That's only a figure of speech," she said.

"Who did kill him?"

She faced him. "You lack sympathy."

"It's not a quality I need."

After a few seconds she said, "This is probably going to sound . . . strange. I suppose, actually, that's one of the reasons I didn't say anything at the time. I just got out of there, because I also had a strong desire not to get involved. You see, I had just landed my skycar—a very lovely mint-green one Leo gave me on my last birthday—on his landing area. The door to his home gym was standing open . . . that was odd, because he was very cautious about keeping the house locked up tight. I . . . I was climbing out of my car and . . . and all at once a man came running from the gym. He ran to the brix wall that surrounded Leo's estate, climbed up it and was over and gone. I—"

"Hold it, sister." Jolson pointed at her with his stogie. "Thackamason had a security system. Wouldn't an alarm have gone off when this bozo went scampering over—"

"There most certainly should've been an alarm, yes. In fact, if he'd come in that way, over the wall, he ought to have gotten a pretty severe shock. An alarm buzzer would have gone off and lights would have flashed inside the house. There's also a guard robot—Leo gave him the nickname Sluggo—who patrols the wall, and he should've stopped the man before he ever touched the wall."

"None of that happened, huh?"

"Not as far as I know."

"Takes damn sophisticated equipment to futz up a complex setup like Thackamason seems to have had."

Mary Jane touched the controls again and the snow returned.

"This next part is even stranger," she said, lowering her voice. "I really don't believe I'm going goofy, Mr. Killdozer. Yet I kept quiet for fear someone might believe I was. But keeping this bottled up hasn't done me much good and I . . . I decided to tell someone. Although I had expected a private investigator to be more—"

"Who was it you saw running out of there?"

She replied, "It was Simon Lenz."

After a slow puff of his cigar, Jolson said, "The guy who invented PlazHartz hearts and founded the whole damn company. The guy who was killed a couple years back. That Simon Lenz?"

"You see, that's why I've refrained from mentioning this," she said. "There's something else unusual, too."

"Spill it."

"It was Simon Lenz," Mary Jane said slowly. "Except that . . . he was much younger. Not more than thirty or so."

"Then it wasn't Lenz. He's got a son named Brian who's about that—"

"It wasn't Brian Lenz. Brian's a husky boy and he has dark hair, not his father's red hair and freckles," she said, frowning. "No, I'm certain this was Simon Lenz, but somehow a Simon Lenz twenty-five years younger."

Jolson asked her, "What else did you see?"

"Nothing."

"You went inside, you saw his body."

"I did, yes. He was . . . lying on the gym floor, wearing a two-piece workout suit, and he had . . . that terrible hole in his chest."

"What about servants?"

"I didn't see any. I . . . I was very afraid and . . . I didn't want to get mixed up in that. Leo still had a wife, even though she lives most of the time on Murdstone in the Barnum System. I simply went away." She lowered her head.

Jolson dug out the list the client had given him. "Did you know Roger Bumlin and Eleanor Ladysmith?"

"I've met Roger a few times at parties. He's in charge of research and design at Plaz," she replied. "I heard Eleanor was killed in some kind of accident a couple weeks ago. I didn't really know her at— My goodness! Is Roger dead, too?"

"Yeah."

"Is that a list of names?"

He tossed it to her. "Might be a list of people who're going to get killed," he said. "How many of the rest of them do you know?"

She scanned the thirteen names. "I've met most of them, through Leo," she said. "All of them, as you must know, work at PlazHartz. Dr. Heather Windom has run the whole operation since Simon Lenz died. And this girl —Carrie Tinsley. She used to be engaged to Brian Lenz, but then he . . . after his father died, he went to seed. They haven't been an item for some time."

"Besides working at PlazHartz, what else do they have in common?"

"Not a thing that I . . ." She paused, lowered the sheet of faxpaper to her lap. "That's odd."

"What, angel?"

"It just occurred to me," she said, "that once—months ago—Leo mentioned several of these people. He'd been using a nasal brainstim spray at a party and was not exactly himself. A party at Dr. Windom's, in fact. I was piloting his skycar home and he . . . this was very unusual for him . . . he began crying. He told me it was very rough to carry guilt around, even when you had a lot of others to help you. He muttered several of these people's names. I'm certain."

"What was he guilty about?"

"I don't know. He'd never talk about it after that and he told me to drop the whole matter. I did, since he wasn't a man you wanted to anger."

"Could they have been involved in Simon Lenz's death?"

"That was an accident, wasn't it?"

Jolson stood, dropping his cigar into the floor dispozhole. "Do you know Jennifer Lenz?"

"Not at all. The poor child had already suffered her breakdown before I became Leo's friend. I understand she was a very intelligent young lady, attractive in a shy sort of way."

"Did Thackamason ever talk about her?"

Mary Jane said, "I know Leo was concerned about Jennifer, although he never actually visited her at that grim asylum she was committed to after her collapse. Sick people upset him, tough as he was, and he shied away from going to hospitals or rest homes. He did tell me that she was, like her father, very gifted as a technician. Her specialty, though, was androids, and I think she'd perfected a much more efficient type shortly before her father's death. After that her illness put a stop to all her work."

Bending, he retrieved the list off her lap and replaced

it with a gloprint business card. "If you think of anything else, sister, give me a holler on the pixie."

Mary Jane left her chair to escort him to the door. "I don't feel much better, Mr. Killdozer, for having confided in you."

"It happens that way sometimes," he said, leaving.

CHAPTER 9

Jolson flipped the listening device to Sally as she came into the apartment. "This yours?"

Dropping the sincloth shopping bag she was carrying, the husky lady detective caught the gadget. "What the heck are you gassing about, Jolson?"

"Spy device," he said, shutting the door of Killdozer's apartment and returning to the lemon-yellow Lucite arm-chair he'd been sitting in when she'd let herself into the place. "I found it in Lou's bedroom, under a pile of linge-rie."

"Lingerie? Are you trying to imply that my boy was—"

"Souvenirs, I imagine."

Sally rubbed her blunt fingertips over the bug. "I don't get any of this," she said. "Who could get in here to plant—"

"You just did."

"I'm his mother. The whorlock accepts my fingerprints as well as Lou's."

Jolson tapped his fingers, which were now tipped with exact replicas of Killdozer's prints, on his chair arm. "While I'm residing in this apartment, Sally, get into the habit of knocking before you barge—"

"You planning to hold whoopee parties or put the boots to—"

"Knock first," he advised, rising.

She placed the bug atop a floating silver-plated end table, stooped, grunting, and grasped up the sack. "I brought you over some chow, since I know Lou was always forgetting to stock up on—"

"The O'Brine case isn't what you and Molly expected." He followed her over the lavender glofloor into the red-and-white kitchen area.

"Doesn't that verdant bastard want to hire Daredevils, Ltd. to do the security work for PlazHartz?"

"Nope."

Crouching in front of the squat green refrigerator, she requested, "Open up, Elmo."

"Ump," said the refrigerator, popping its door open.

"Nothing but three plazcanz of near beer and some grout cheese dip that looks fuzzy. He's going to get— Hell, I keep forgetting he's dead." She shoved the whole shopping bag in, not bothering to unpack. "Shut yourself, Elmo. What does O'Brine want, then?"

"He's afraid he's going to be murdered."

"Cripes," Sally remarked, settling into a neon kitchen chair. "We can't soak him much more than a thousand trubux a day and expenses for a job like that."

Jolson said, "You better get a coded hypergram off to Molly and explain the setup. She may not think it's worth my staying—"

"Wait now, Jolson." She stood, took hold of his arm. "We can still maybe make a bundle of dough out of this caper. Sure. If we keep this green gink from getting iced, he'll be grateful. We'll nudge him into hiring us to do all the security work for PlazHartz. See, the detective business just requires one hell of a lot of—"

"Patience. I know," he said. "You didn't have any notion he was worried about his life?"

"I didn't know diddly about O'Brine."

"According to him, three important PlazHartz executives have already been murdered. He's sure he's also on the list."

"Who does he think drew up that list?"

"Claims he doesn't know. But it could be he suspects somebody who was close to Simon Lenz."

Returning to the refrigerator, she said, "Open again, Elmo."

"Urp."

"Simon Lenz?" She reached into the sack, pulled free a bunch of blue carrots. "That's the galoot who ran Plaz-Hartz."

"Up until he ceased to be, yep." He watched her carry the carrots to the sink. "Lou never mentioned any of this?"

"He kept his cases to himself. Alls I know, like I already told you, is that he had a series of appointments with O'Brine." She dumped the carrots into the left-hand bin of the sink and told it, "Wash and dice these, huh?"

"Do you know anything about Jennifer Lenz?"

"Absolutely zero. Who the heck is she?"

"Simon's daughter. How about Brian Lenz?"

"The son maybe?" Sally shook her head. "Never heard of him."

He asked her, "Who else is interested in this case?"

"Want me to fix you some carrot soup?"

"No."

Turning her back to the sink, she said, "Could be I'm

a little dense, Jolson. But I don't get what you're asking me."

"Somebody's been trying real hard to find out what I'm up to," he reminded her. "Thus far they've only planted bugs."

"I got no idea who—"

"You've been jumpy yourself," he went on. "Sidetracking me so we could meet in Basher Park instead of the Daredevils, Ltd. offices. Acting like I was Lou back from the dead when I walked into your office. The whole—"

"You've obviously never been a mother," she said, growing angry. "Losing Lou was like getting booted in the breadbasket." She looked right at him. "That's why I been acting edgy, Jolson."

He nodded. "You better go home and get that message off to Molly Briggs."

"What are you going to do next?"

"I'll emulate Lou," he said, taking her by the arm and leading her out of the kitchen and toward the exit, "and keep that to myself."

The computer terminal was in a bad mood. It muttered, turned its display screen a bile green, fidgeted on its stand. "What kind of scam you trying to pull, Lou?" its voxbox inquired.

"C'mon, quit being a meathead." Jolson was sitting on the edge of a purple hiphug chair in Killdozer's purple-walled den. "Give me what you've got on the Wally O'Brine case."

"What you got to do, fella, is slip me the access password," said the terminal. "Like I told your mom couple days ago, when she tried to get me to spill the same beans: no password, no info."

"It's me." Jolson held up a hand to the screen. "The boss."

"Lou, baby, don't make me recite the basic laws of robotics to—"

"You're not a robot."

"Same as, far as the laws of handing over info without proper—"

"Listen, crumbum, I just forgot the damn word. I got hit on the noggin couple times yesterday while investigating—"

"No dice, Lou. Ask me another."

Jolson slouched. "Okay," he said, taking out the list the gatorman had given him and holding it up to the terminal's scanner. "I want BG reports on all of these people. Boil each entry down to fifteen hundred words tops, but include everything they have in common. Anything that links them together I want. Can you do that without any more futzing around?"

"A cinch. Give me about fifteen—"

The pixphone in the alcove across the room had started buzzing.

"Get started." He crossed to the phone. "Yeah?"

The small rectangular pixscreen stayed dark for a few seconds. Then a thin, black-haired young woman appeared. "Wonderful," she said disdainfully in a somewhat nasal voice. "There must be something in the power of prayer after all, because I've been praying that I'd get hold of you eventually so I could ask you what in the hell you—"

"Hold it, sweetheart," he told her. "No need to get nasty with Lou Killdozer."

There was only darkness behind the young woman and Jolson couldn't tell where she was calling from. On top of that, he had no idea who she was. Her face hadn't been included in any of his briefing material.

"Do we still have a deal or not?" she asked.

"I never go back on my word. You ought to know that."

"Why? Until a week ago, when you came nosing around asking rude questions about Brian, I'd never laid eyes on you before," she said. "And what I'd heard of you didn't exactly convince me you—"

"Angel, a deal's a deal."

"If that's so, Lou, why is it I haven't heard from you for days?"

"You got a perfect right to ask that." He tugged out a vile cigar, lit it.

"What I told you about, the special lead I gave you, that's something that can turn into a lot of money," she said. "Money for both of us if we play certain people at PlazHartz just right. I've been wondering, though, if you aren't planning to cut me out."

"Didn't I give you my word you'd share in the take, Carrie?" he said, taking a chance that this was Brian Lenz's former lady friend.

"You did, Lou, yes. You also assured me you'd call me back the next day."

So she was Carrie Tinsley, who still worked for Plaz-Hartz. And who was, though she probably didn't know it, on the list of possible murder victims.

"Listen, angel cake, the detecting business isn't like making imitation organs," he said, blowing out smoke. "When I get to digging, it takes—"

"Have you been able to confirm anything I told you about?"

He waggled his left hand in the air. "Things are moving

along," he said. "Tell you what, Carrie. Why don't I come over right now so we can—"

"Not here, no."

"You look kind of scared, kid. But with Lou Killdozer in your corner, you got—"

"Of course I'm scared. I told you that last time," the dark-haired girl said impatiently. "I also told you it wasn't a good idea for you to be seen anywhere near my home. I think someone may be watching this—"

"Pick a place that's safe. Ditch any tails and—"

"Meet me at the Derelict in two hours," said Carrie. "Be damn careful, too, Lou. Don't so much as approach me unless it looks absolutely safe."

"Don't worry, sugar."

"Two hours." The screen went black.

"Where's the Derelict?" he asked the computer terminal.

"Do you want the scoop on these clunks or do you want the address of some second-rate orbiting night spot?"

"Both," said Jolson. "Fast."

CHAPTER 10

A thick night mist hung over the parking area behind the apartment complex. Downhill, foghorns were hooting on the bay.

Jolson, wearing an orange-hued neowool trench coat, crossed the pastel plazgravel to Killdozer's landcar.

Buster the robot was sitting in the driveseat.

Easing into the backseat, Jolson said, "Where can I catch a shuttle for a place called the Derelict?" He reached over to tug the door shut, but it slammed itself before he touched it and locked with a heavy click.

The engine growled to life, and the landcar started rushing backwards toward the exit gate.

"Buster, what are you up to?"

The robot didn't reply.

Stretching, Jolson saw that Buster had his hands folded in his lap. The vehicle was driving itself.

Jolson took hold of his door's lock release and yanked. The door didn't budge.

The car went bouncing, bottom whapping the roadway, out of the lot and spun around. They started racing downhill, aiming at the fog-shrouded bay a half mile away.

"Killdozer?" came a gruff voice out of the voxbox on the dash.

"Yeah?" He jerked a kilgun from his trench coat pocket.

"You don't learn so good."

"Meaning what, meathead?"

"We told you once to lay off and forget all about Plaz-Hartz."

"Nobody tells Lou Killdozer what to do." He braced himself against the far side of the car, fired at the door.

The weapon failed to function at all.

"We warn you once, Killdozer. Next we fix you." The voxbox went dead.

Jolson raised a booted foot, kicked several times, hard, at the shatterproof glaz window. It didn't shatter.

The car was moving ever faster. The bay was less than a hundred yards away and they were obviously heading for a pieramp that stretched out some five hundred feet over the water.

Jolson's final destination seemed obvious.

He kicked at the lock.

Outside the window he saw another landcar, gleaming crimson, racing along beside his runaway. The blanked windows kept him from seeing who was in it.

His car hit the pier, the ribbed surface making the wheels hum, and rushed on.

Jolson estimated he was about fifteen seconds from diving into the bay.

He felt an odd twisting pain start spreading from his midsection through his entire body.

Then he wasn't in the car any longer. He was sprawled on a stretch of sandy beach watching it sail clear of the end of the pier and go plummeting into the black water.

There was an enormous splash. The water and the fog closed in and the night quiet returned.

"Boy, you pay three hundred sixty thousand dollars for a thingamajig and then it almost doesn't work on you. I tell you, Ben, I was awfully worried there for a minute."

"I was a mite concerned myself, Molly," he acknowledged, starting up the gritty green sand to where the red-haired young woman stood beside the parked crimson car. "How'd you get here?"

"Followed you from the Killdozer apartment, and a darn good thing, too," she said. "Did I happen to mention to you back home on Barnum that this new wallwalker I'm wearing also has a teleport unit built in? Well, it does. That was handy, because I used it to pluck you right out of the death car. Once, that is, I realized you weren't just joyriding and being silly."

"I seldom am silly these days. And when I am, it doesn't involve driving into deep bodies of water."

"That's exactly what I concluded." Smiling, she patted her stomach. "Of course, driving an unfamiliar rental car at breakneck speed while trying to aim a portable teleport beam isn't that easy, especially when the darn thing's strapped to your tummy and you have to read all the dials sort of upside down and backwards."

"I'm grateful." Putting an arm around her slim waist, he kissed Molly on the cheek. "Thanks."

"You sure smell like cheap cigars. Oh, but I suppose that's all part of the—"

"Why are you on this particular planet?"

"Good thing I am, don't you think?"

"I do, except I left you back on—"

"I thought I mentioned I might pop up here on Farpa —actually I took the next hyperspace liner after yours—

to see how you were getting on," Molly explained. "That's a dreadful overcoat, by the way."

"It is, yes," he agreed. "Could you do me one further favor?"

"Why, certainly, Ben. Even though, technically, I'm your employer and superior, I've always felt we were good friends and—"

"There's a robot still in the car. Can you fish him out with that thing?"

"Don't see why not." She studied him, head tilted slightly. "Are you getting sentimental already about the sidekicks you've picked up in the brief time you've—"

"I want to find out what he knows about this attempt to do me in."

"Oh, yes, right," said Molly. "That is something we have to find out about."

Jolson glanced around the domed living room of the bayside villa. "Impressive," he said. "Does this go on your Briggs Interplanetary Detective Service expense account?"

Molly was frowning at the damp footprints Buster was tracking across the thick off-white carpeting. "There's not one single five-star hotel in this entire planet system, according to *Galactic Michelin*," she informed him. "Precious few that rate four. Besides which, I'd feel darn embarrassed walking across a crowded hotel lobby with a waterlogged mechanical man and you in that god-awful overcoat."

"I'm completely presentable, lady," insisted Buster, halting in front of the fireplace to hold out his soggy sleeves to the electrologs. "But, say, boss, let me apologize again for letting youse down."

"What you have to do, Buster, is tell me what you saw before they used the disabler on you."

The robot shook his round head, causing drops of water to splat against the pale grey wall. "I been trying, but so far I'm drawing a blank."

Slipping free of the orange trench coat, Jolson dropped it over the back of a black slingchair. "Sit on yonder sofa," he ordered the robot. "I'll fiddle with your inner workings and see—"

"Nix, Jolson. I don't like even youse to go monkeying with my—"

"Nevertheless." From his coat pocket he produced a small multitool.

"Ben, that suit's even worse than the coat." Molly perched on the edge of a grey floating coffee table.

"I been meaning to mention that the quiff ought to get into the habit of calling youse Lou," said Buster. "So as not to blow the impersonation."

"Space lag probably affects her thinking equipment. She means well."

"Aw, that's always the trouble with organic brains."

"At least no one," pointed out Molly, crossing her slim legs, "snuck up on me and used a disabler. I mean, you'd think a bodyguard—a heck of an expensive one from what I recall reading in the Daredevils, Ltd. annual report— ought to be able to—"

"Let's observe a moment of silence." Jolson had the mechanical man's metal chest open and was probing with the tip of the multitool.

"Ouch," complained Buster. "Feels like you hit my crazy bone."

After a few minutes of tinkering, Jolson closed up the

chest panel. "Okay, that ought to do it," he announced. "Now tell us what happened."

The robot leaned back on the black sofa. "I can remember," he said, pleased. "Except, boss, there ain't that much to remember."

"Give me what you've got."

"I only heard them. They must of been in a skycar," Buster recounted. "It come down from right overhead of me and the buggy. Before I could even pile out to take a gander—*zzzzitttttzzzzz!*—a disabler beam. I conked out. When I wake up, I'm soaking wet and you and this jane tell me I took a dip in the bay."

"Anything else?"

Buster considered. "I got me a very dim recollection of a skinny birdman in a two-piece dark cazsuit fooling with the dash. That was after I'd been zapped, though, and I can't swear to nothing."

Jolson stood back. "Buster, I made a few basic changes in your workings," he told the robot. "From now on you report only to me."

"That's what I always—"

"Only to me, and only when I give you the password, which happens to be *chameleon.*"

"Very original," murmured Molly.

"You can leave right now. Get back to Daredevils, Ltd. and get yourself another car," said Jolson. "Your full-time assignment, Buster, is to tag Sally. Follow her, keep track of what she does, where she goes, whom she sees."

"You want me to tail Lou's old lady?"

"That I do. I'll contact you in the landcar to get your reports. Don't let Sally know you're around."

"I'm a whiz at tailing. But the idea of—"

"You just have to do it."

Buster reflected. "Yeah, you did diddle me up inside. And I do got to."

"Get started."

The big robot left the sofa, trudged for the door. "Anyways, thanks again for rescuing me from a watery grave, one and all."

"You're welcome," called Molly as the front door opened and shut and Buster stepped out into the misty night. "Ben, could you maybe now explain what the heck is going on around here?"

"First I have to make a call to postpone a meeting with a lady."

"Can't your social life wait until—"

"This is Lou Killdozer's business life," he said. "It begins to look as though Daredevils, Ltd. isn't the spotless, true-blue agency you and your dad thought you were buying."

"Is this more Jolson cynicism or do you—"

"I'll give you what facts I have shortly." He spotted the pixphone alcove, walked over. "We have considerable to talk about."

"So I gather. Do you really have to light one of those awful cigars?"

"Part of the act." He puffed on the fresh stogie while punching out the number the computer terminal in Killdozer's apartment had provided him with.

"Hello?" It was a rumbling masculine voice and the screen stayed black.

"Put Carrie on the phone, chum."

"Suppose, Lou, you first tell me why you're calling the lady?" A thickset lizardman in a three-piece tan bizsuit appeared on the phone screen.

"Well, if it isn't Lieutenant Fairball." The homicide

squad officer Jolson remembered from his briefing. "What's happening?"

"You know Carrie Tinsley?"

"Recently met her in the course of an investigation. Right now I'm just following up a routine—"

"She's dead, Lou," the lizard cop told him.

"Any idea who killed her?"

"We don't know," said Fairball. "This case you're working on—would there be a lean red-haired kid, freckled and about twenty years old, involved?"

Jolson leaned closer to the screen. "You got a witness?"

"Maybe somebody saw something, maybe not. Well?"

"Tomorrow sometime," Jolson promised, "I'll come in and let down my hair with you, Lieutenant."

"Do that, because I hate to pay all the overtime to the boys I'll send out to drag your toke in here if you don't show." The phone screen returned to black.

Jolson moved away, tossed the cigar in the nearest dispozhole. "Setbacks," he said, shaking his head. "A lot of them so far."

"Who was Carrie Tinsley?"

"A lady who might've known more about what's going on than we do." He cocked his head in the direction of the sofa. "Sit and I'll fill you in."

"Are you really intending to go in and talk to the local police tomorrow?"

"It might be useful, but I'm not sure," he answered. "I may want to stop being Lou Killdozer for a while."

"Because they're trying to kill you?"

"That's one good reason," he admitted.

CHAPTER 11

Molly sighed and slumped further on the black sofa. "I'm not liking the sound of any of this."

Himself again, Jolson was pacing the villa living room. "Maybe the best course of action," he suggested, "is to unload the Killdozer agency and hop on the next liner out."

"No, we don't operate that way." She sat up, frowning. "If Lou and his mother are crooked, then we have to make certain of the fact. And, since BIDS is now responsible for Daredevils, Ltd., we have to solve this murder case, save the client's life and tie up any and all loose ends. We have our reputation across the universe to think about."

"I'm not sure about Strangler Sally yet, but it looks like Lou was definitely involved in some kind of blackmail deal with the late Carrie Tinsley."

"Darn, and they put out such an impressive annual report." Molly shook her head. "Okay, what do we do next?"

"Possibly you still book passage for home while I—"

"Nope, I'm sticking. One of the things Dad taught me was—"

"If you stay, I still have to be in charge."

"Aren't we equals, partners? Have I, so far, thrown my weight around or reminded you that I co-own one of the largest—"

"So far, no. However, in the past you—"

"The past is over and done. I know, yes, that when we worked together last, on Barafunda in the Barnum System, I did act sort of bossy. I'm more mature now."

Jolson eyed her. "I want to find out who tried to kill Lou."

"This last time, you mean?"

"This last time may be the only time."

"Just because Sally sent me cigar ashes instead of Lou's true remains doesn't mean he didn't sink into that swamp."

"Doesn't mean he did either."

"Well, we won't squabble over that point just now."

Still pacing, he said, "I'd like to talk to Brian Lenz. And it'd be helpful to know where Jennifer Lenz is at this moment."

"Brian was engaged to Carrie once, so he might just know what she and Lou were up to. Can't bank on it, though."

"He must know some basic Lenz family secrets. For instance, I'm wondering if either Simon or Jennifer ever built some android sims of the senior Lenz."

Snapping her fingers, Molly said, "Replicas of Simon Lenz at different ages, you mean?"

"I do, yep."

"That could be what these witnesses have been seeing." After bouncing twice, she recrossed her legs. "The killer always looks like Simon Lenz, except they can't agree on his age. One claims twenty, the other thirty."

"Android killers are a possibility."

"But if that's true, Ben, then somebody in the Lenz family has to be responsible—either Brian or Jennifer."

"Or that's what somebody else would like us to think."

"If the reason all thirteen of those people got on the list is because they're involved in Simon Lenz's death, then it stands to reason either—"

"They could be on the list because they're responsible; they could be on the list because O'Brine thinks they are," he said. "It's also possible that's not the reason at all for their being killed off."

Molly paused to consider that. "Yes, I guess we have to be patient," she said finally. "That, after all, is what investigative work is—"

"Right now I'm heading into some of the Danger Zones in the capital," he said. "You'd better—"

"Hey, haven't I ever showed you my ID packet? I'm a fully licensed private operative." Molly rose to her feet. "There's no place I'm afraid to go in the line of duty."

He grinned. "We'll depart, then."

"What new identity are you—"

"Go as myself for a while, since I haven't been in the Hellquads for a few years," he answered. "Seems a lot safer than trying Lou or even Humazoo."

"Now . . . wait a sec." She made a come-here motion at him. "Lean over toward me, tilt your head down."

"Hmm?" He complied with her request.

"No bald spot anymore. I thought I'd noticed that earlier."

"After our conversation in my warehouse, I decided that letting myself go bald was an affectation."

"I'm glad you're starting to heed my advice."

"A little of it," he said.

The three-car landtrain shuddered, slowed, produced several new mournful whines, swayed and came to a stuttering halt.

"Gumpox grumble grumble," announced the overhead dangling comsystem speaker.

Molly rubbed the heel of her hand over the fogged glaz of the window. "I know I've made this same assumption the last three times we lurched to a halt—but could this be the Danger Zone #26 station?"

Jolson looked out the window with her. "Yep, I think it—"

"Grumble grumb . . . WHOP! There, that's better. DZ26, end of line," announced the ceiling voxbox. "Thanks for riding with the HQSTS. Have a nice evening, although that seems highly unlikely under the circumstances. End of the line."

Taking Molly's arm, Jolson escorted her through the otherwise empty Hellquad Quaint & Slow Transit System car. "Cling to me from here on out."

She disengaged herself and stepped out into the night. "I can fend for myself, Ben."

The platform was made of dying neowood and the evening fog hung thick all around. The tiny train station huddled to their left, unlit and tumbledown.

One of the several dark mounds scattered across the swayback planks suddenly stood, turned into a ragged catman and came lurching toward Molly.

"Pretty lady, can you spare a trubuck for . . ." He toppled face forward, hit the misty platform with a furry thump and remained sprawled there.

"I wonder," said Molly, stepping carefully around him, "what he wanted the dollar for."

Jolson took hold of her arm again. "We go along that street over there." He led her toward the twisted sudoiron stairway and then down to the dark street twenty feet below. "When we come to the First Church of Saint Serpentine, we turn right."

Shivering, she hunched her shoulders slightly. "You really don't think we can trust the Daredevils, Ltd. computer? That would sure be a heck of a lot easier than hunting all over the—"

"Can't trust the computer any more than we can trust the personnel, living and dead."

The church Jolson remembered from his last trip had long ago become a burned-out ruin. A group was huddled in amongst the blackened remains, passing a plazflask of radiant wine.

The street they walked along was narrow, flanked by thin wedges of buildings. PREACHER O'BRIEN'S SCHOOL FOR HOMELESS HOOLIGANS, announced a flickering glosign on a stunted brix structure. Further along signs read MONKEY SANDWICHES!, INTERPLANETARY BROTHERHOOD OF SMUGGLERS—FARPA CHAPTER, THE RUPERT FFAGIN SCHOOL OF KNAVERY, CLUB MUD, MINT CONDITION BORDELLO—ONLY VIRGINS IN STOCK!, LOWER DEPTHS CAFE II.

Nodding in the direction of this last sign, Jolson said, "We've arrived at our initial destination."

"Just when I was starting to enjoy the sights." She put both hands on his arm.

CHAPTER 12

The bartender had an air-freshener nozzle built into his chrome-plated left hand. After spraying all around their section of the bar, he said, "Sorry the joint smells so bad, Ben. Tonight of all nights. You haven't dropped in for —what is it? Four, five years—and just before you and this personable young lady waltz in, some of these low-life clowns have to set fire to a little old birdwoman. Wow, and nothing smells worse than singed feathers."

"Except that stuff you're squirting us with," mentioned Molly, nose wrinkling. "What is it?"

The cyborg catman put his glittering metal forefinger up near his furry nose and squirted a quick whiff. "That's bug killer—sorry. I was cleaning up the pantry just before you and the looker arrived, Ben. Forgot to switch back."

Jolson rested both elbows on the bar. "I'm hoping you can help me, Bathhouse."

Bathhouse Berrill said, "You still passing out the standard honorarium for useful and pertinent information?"

"Actually it's risen twenty trubux over what it—ow!"

Molly had kicked him. "If you'll submit a voucher for twenty-five trudollars, Mr. Berrill, you'll receive a check in no more than thirty working days."

Bathhouse's yellow eyes narrowed. "Is your companion noted for her whimsy, Ben?"

"To the four corners of the universe, yep." He dropped a hundred trudollars in cash on the dark neowood.

Molly made an unhappy sound and turned her attention to gazing into the cloudy mirror behind the bar. It gave a dim view of the dim-lit little room and the dozen muffled patrons inhabiting the bar and the few ramshackle booths.

"How can I be of . . . Say, miss—it is miss, isn't it? You don't happen to be Mrs. Jolson?"

"I'm not that whimsical," she assured him. "It's miss."

"Excuse my mentioning it, miss, but you seem to be ignoring your drink," said Bathhouse. "That brandy is teleported all the way from the Earth System. It's not local junk."

"The brandy's no doubt fine, but this big lipstick smear on the rim of my glass cooled my enthusiasm."

He picked up the glass in his right hand. "Aw, that isn't lipstick." He chuckled and returned the glass to its place in front of her.

"What, then?"

"Looks very much like crayon to me. What's your guess, Ben?"

"Orange marmalade."

The catman bartender ran his metal forefinger across the stain, then licked at the finger. "Naw, that's sure not jam," he concluded, whiskers waggling. "Pooey, it tastes like bug spray."

"That's because," Jolson pointed out, "you're sampling your bug-spray finger."

"So I am." He picked up the glass, downed the brandy himself. "I'll pour you a new drink in a fresh glass, miss. On the house."

"No need," she said.

"At least partake of some of the popcorn in the bowl there. We pop it ourselves in the pantry."

"It appears to be burned."

"What?" Bathhouse brought the red plaz bowl up close to his face. "Aw, that's only a few burned feathers on the top."

"Bathhouse," said Jolson in a more confidential tone, "I want to contact Dr. IQ."

The bartender said, "Never much liked that guy. Hate to think it's bigotry or—"

"Where can I find him?"

"He's got a new place just off Sodomy Lane, about two miles south of here," said the cyborg, scratching his furry left ear with his metal thumb. "Let me see . . . address is #203A Bondage Alley."

"We'll call on him." Jolson swung off the stool.

"Drop in again before you leave our little planet," invited the bartender. "Couple more nights and the smell'll be gone."

When Molly's nose gave another involuntary twitch, she rubbed the palm of her hand across the tip and remarked, "It's really too bad we can't use our own computer."

Jolson was leaning against the wall of the small, soot-colored room and watching the ratman who sat huddled at the considerably unorthodox computer terminal at the room's center. "We can't trust it," he reminded.

"Ar, it's no doubt me personally the young lady doesn't care for," suggested the thin, scruffy ratman. "I'm used to that, Ben. Such attitudes don't ruffle my—"

"She's got nothing against you, Dr. IQ."

"Nice of you to try soothing my feelings," he said, cheek whiskers quivering. "But, let's face it, most people, especially humanoids, don't care for rats. You can point out to them until you're blue in the fur that a rat and a ratperson aren't the same at all. But, alas, there does happen to be that unfortunate resemblance."

"And there's all this cheese." Molly, arms folded and knees pressed tight together, was sitting on a crippled sofa. Nearby rose a wall of shelves that held dozens of wedges of cheese on small pastel plaz plates.

"Ar, that's true enough, Miss Briggs," admitted IQ. "Rats, those disgusting little vermin, do show a fondness for cheese. But allow me to point out that many gourmets of all sorts do as well. For instance, I was noticing only the other evening in a vidbook entitled *Eating Cheese to Win,* written by a most respected author, not a ratman either but a best-selling toadman, the interesting statistic that—"

"Doc, we're paying you to tap into some information sources," reminded Jolson. "Forget about defending your ethnic—"

"Right you are, Ben." The hunched ratman adjusted his grey knit cap with his mittened hands. "Oh, by the way, miss, feel free to help yourself to any and all of the cheeses while you're waiting—some Gruyère, Schwarzenberger, Camembert, Spitzkase, or pimento perhaps. Myself, I'm especially fond of Gorgonzola."

"I ate a lot of popcorn just before coming here," she said. "Thanks all the same."

"Well, back to the clandestine gathering of data." His mittens made a dull rasping sound as he rubbed his hands together. He started whapping at the unconventional keyboard. "Here comes some of what you want. Brian Lenz has been living off in a run-down satellite that orbits Farpa for the past four and one half months." He touched at the information crawling across the streaked display screen. "He's shacked up with— Excuse my lingo, Miss Briggs. Brian appears to be cohabiting with a lady juggler who was earning quite a reputation here in the territory as a comedy personality until her fondness for the drug zombium began affecting her timing. I can retrieve some of her notices should—"

"Won't be necessary. Her name's Margo McQuest, huh?" Jolson was reading over the ratman's narrow shoulder.

"Stage name."

"What are they up to on the satellite?"

"That's just rolling by now," said Dr. IQ. "This satellite has been dubbed the Little Theater Off Planet. A whole gaggle of supposedly rehabilitated troupers reside there and put on plays and shows. The reviews of their latest effort, entitled *What's the Meaning of It All?*, have been pretty favorable. For example, Jack Fuller in the *Farpa Shopping News* says, 'I sat spellbound as this trenchant—' "

"Brian's pixphone calls," cut in Jolson, who was pacing the ashen rug. "Can you get a list of them for the past few weeks? Also whether he's left that floating opera house and paid any visits to Farpa."

"Piece of cheese, as they say. No trouble," Dr. IQ assured him. "But it'll take a couple of hours, since I have to dodge certain safeguards put in place by outfits like the Hellquad Communications Authority and—"

"You can start on that after we leave and I'll get it from you tomorrow," said Jolson. "Next get me a location for Jennifer Lenz."

"Isn't she," asked Molly, unfolding and refolding her arms, "locked safely away at some institution or other?"

"That's what I want to confirm," he said. "She was supposed to be very devoted to her father, and it could be she's now devoted to revenging herself on everybody who did him wrong."

"If anybody did. You're only guessing about that, Ben."

"Yep, playing a hunch."

"How about a pat of Brie cheese on a Galactic Ritz cracker?" the ratman asked Molly.

"Pass."

"This isn't the sloppy, runny sort of Brie. It's a fairly new variation, made of grout milk and—"

"To work, Doc," urged Jolson.

"Ar, sorry." He fingered several keys. "Funny. Most funny."

"What?"

"Some sort of block's been put up—recently—an extra block on Jennifer Lenz's files at the Madhouse Spa over in Laguna Territory."

"Can you get around it?"

"Should be able to." He ran his mittened hands over the keyboard, hunched lower in his chair. "Wellsir, just look at that, Ben. Turns out she's not there at all."

"She isn't?" Molly stood, nearly knocking a plate of green cheese off the end table.

"According to the asylum records, Jennifer Lenz somehow escaped from the place seven weeks ago."

"Before," said Molly, "the murders started."

"Before, yeah."

"Funny," muttered Dr. IQ.

"Something else?"

"These entries about her escape . . ." The ratman

shrugged. "They don't ring quite true. Can't exactly tell you why, though."

"You think they're faked some way?"

"I just feel something's not quite right."

"Can you poke around further?"

"That'll take time, too."

"Okay, then let me give you one more thing to work on before we go," said Jolson. "See if you can find out who's trying to kill Lou Killdozer."

The high, wide gate recognized Molly's voice and slid open. She drove the crimson landcar onto the grounds of her rented villa and parked in a garage pod. "I thought detectives never slept," she said as she eased out of the driveseat, "while caught up in a case."

"Dim-witted ones maybe." Jolson strolled down to the one-way seethru wall bordering the bay.

The fog was still heavy over the night water.

"Would you like me to fix you a hot cup of carobsub before you turn in, Ben?" She came and stood near him.

"Nope."

"No trouble, because there's a machine that does just and only that in the vast kitchen here. Costs twelve hundred sixty trudollars—at least back on Barnum."

"Tomorrow," he said, "you'll set up an appointment with one of the surviving PlazHartz executives on our list. Try to get in and see him sometime tomorrow."

"Him?"

"Be handier if it's a male, one who finds you moderately attractive."

"There should be at least one out of the ten left."

"Nine left," he corrected. "We have to cross Carrie

Tinsley off. Get this PlazHartz survivor to invite you to dinner."

"Someplace quiet, where you can slip in and question him?"

Jolson nodded. "Someplace where I can maybe use a truthdisc on him and get him to tell all he knows."

"Actually I won't tell him we suspect a murder plot," she said. "No, my story is—I'm the new owner of Dare-devils, Ltd., which is now a branch of BIDS. Happened to be visiting his planet and wanted to give him the opportunity to hire us to take over PlazHartz security work. Hand him a tri-op brochure, copy of our ten-minute vidcaz pitch."

"That ought to work."

"I'm a pretty good salesperson," she said. "We might really get the darn account."

Jolson started for the villa. "Be careful, though."

"You don't trust the PlazHartz folks either."

"Safer not to trust anybody," he said. "When I get more information from Dr. IQ tomorrow and find out who tried to kill Lou tonight, then maybe I can start making a list of trustworthy people."

Molly followed him into the living room through the sliding doors. "You really think that run-down ratman can find out who—"

"Dr. IQ's good, don't underestimate him." Jolson sat in a black slingchair. "His dietary habits have clouded your judgment."

"Oh, and that's another thing I meant to point out." She dropped onto the sofa and faced him. "You must've known I was anxious to get out of his smelly hideaway, yet you sat there and shared a plate of cheese and crackers with—"

"Diplomacy. It's important in our work, Molly."

"That one cheese had, I swear, squiggly little bugs living in it."

"While you're infiltrating PlazHartz, I'm going to visit Brian Lenz and find out where his missing sister is."

"You mean you don't wish to work as a team any longer?"

"We are a team. Part of the team handles one job, part another."

"My notion of teamwork is more a side-by-side thing."

"We differ."

"Suppose they try to kill you again?"

"So far it's Lou they've been trying to terminate. And I'm not going to be him for a spell."

"It would still be better if I were hanging around in the background, ready to—"

"Most times I can save myself." He rose. "Which guest room is mine?"

She watched him for a moment. "Whichever one you like," she said finally. "I'll be in the master bedroom."

"I figured that," he said.

"Good night," she said.

CHAPTER 13

"A fate worse than death," the slim young woman with rainbow hair was explaining to Jolson.

He was still himself, sharing a seat with her on the dingy, moderately crowded morning shuttle carrying them up to the orbiting Little Theater Off Planet. "Try to look on the positive side, Miss . . ."

"Shoot, I forgot to introduce myself. Talk about publicity sense." From the big globead purse resting on her narrow lap she fished a thick business card to hand to him.

"INTRODUCING," bellowed the talking card, "MISS TIMMY TEMPEST, REPORTER AT LARGE FOR *GALACTIC VARIETY!*"

The card, which was glowing a rich scarlet, kept getting increasingly warm in Jolson's hand. He dropped it to the cabin floor.

"Shoot." Timmy bent and, gingerly, plucked it up between thumb and forefinger. "They've been doing that of late, overheating. It's the batteries or something."

"INTRODUCING MISS TIMMY—"

"Enough, enough." She shut the booming business card away in her purse. "Anyhow, I've been with this rag for over seven weeks and they still keep sending me out on nothing but dippy second-rate assignments. Face it, doing a hundred and fifty words on the cast of a satirical review called *What's the Meaning of It All?* isn't going to win me the accolades of—"

"Hey, cutie pie, I got a helluva scoop for you." Directly across the aisle sat an unkempt lizardman in a frayed two-piece fog-grey cazsuit. He held a small seethru plazbox on one knee.

"Look at this stiff," said Timmy to Jolson. "A washed-up and over-the-hill talent agent from the looks of him, making one last desperate attempt to place some dippy act with these dimbulbs up on this rattletrap satellite we're heading for."

"Babe, that's exactly my situation," admitted the lizardman, grinning broadly. "Allow me to introduce myself. I'm out of business cards, since I neglected to call on my electronics shop this A.M. I am, nevertheless, Glenn Zipp."

"Oh, glory," commented Timmy, smirking. "What a phony name that is. Glenn Zipp. Hooey."

"You're heartless, which is only to be expected with eager, upwardly mobile young humanoids in the field of entertainment journalism," said Zipp amiably. "Be that as it may, Timmy honey, I am going to give you the chance to interview the hottest new singing group in the universe."

"I bet." She nudged Jolson in the ribs. "A broken-down rumdum like you, a washed-up Glenn Zipp, has got the hottest singing group in the uni tied up with an exclusive contract."

"That's exactly the situation, sweetie pie." Zipp leaned further out into the aisle, eying Jolson. "Are you a member of the press as well, old buddy?"

"Just a civilian," Jolson said. "Going up to see about reserving a block of seats for my parents' fiftieth wedding anniv—"

"Oh, glory," Timmy sneered. "You're turning out to be dippier than Zipp."

The green agent proudly held up the plazbox. "Here they are!"

"Here who is?"

"The most terrific vocal group to hit the Hellquads in an eon or more," he explained. "I give you—the Fleas. Go ahead, fellas, make with one of your latest platinum hits."

The rainbow-haired reporter squinted. "Singing fleas— is that what's supposed to be inside the dornick?"

"Sure thing, cutie. C'mon, gang, let's have some warbling." He jiggled the box. "Sometimes their amplifier goes on the—"

"That box is empty," she pointed out.

"Impossible, since I fed the Fleas soon after we embarked on this— Great guns! They're gone." Zipp ceased peering into the empty plazbox and tottered upright. "Stay in your seats, everybody. The hottest singing group of the decade may be underfoot." On hands and knees, he began a slow search of the aisle. "Fellas?"

"What a pathetic old coot," observed Timmy. "Most people get that way once they pass forty."

"All the great journalists," reminded Jolson, "have a sympathetic nature."

"Nertz," said Timmy.

There was a whanging, crunching noise and they entered the dim docking area of the orbiting theater.

Brian Lenz was plump, dark-haired and moderately weary. Seated in a neocanvas chair in the wings, he was watching the brightly lit stage. "That's great, Margo," he called to the husky blue-skinned young woman who was rehearsing her juggling act. "She's good, isn't she?"

Jolson was crouched near a spill of ropes and cables. "Except for the places where she drops things and they break."

"Oh, the mistakes are all part of the act."

"What are those things she's juggling—they look like small statues?"

"Snergs," explained Brian. "We buy them cheap from a discount warehouse down on Farpa. People get a real kick out of seeing snergs smash when she feigns clumsiness. You can only drop two or three per perf. The humor tends to thin if—"

Out on the stage another snerg hit the plazplanks and shattered.

"Six," said Jolson.

"This is only a rehearsal." Brian was still holding the card Jolson had given him a few minutes earlier. "I've heard of the Briggs agency. I don't quite understand why you—"

"We've been retained to investigate the death of Carrie Tinsley," lied Jolson. "Since you—"

"What do you mean, death? Carrie certainly isn't—"

"Last night."

"But I monitor all the newscasts from Farpa, in case anybody plugs the show. I . . ." He rubbed his hand across his forehead. "Why haven't I seen . . . what happened?"

"She was shot, with a kilgun."

"That'd tear a hell of a hole in her." He crumpled Jolson's card. "Carrie was pretty. On the skinny side but . . . why wasn't it on the news?"

"Apparently the PlazHartz organization doesn't want that, which is why our client hired—"

"Are you working for those bastards?"

"Not at all."

"They're bastards. What they did to my father, and then . . ."

"What did they do?"

Brian said, "That has nothing to do with Carrie Tinsley."

Jolson asked him, "When's the last time you saw her?"

"We broke up. Wasn't her fault exactly. I sort of went flooey after my father died." He shifted in his chair, watching the blue-skinned juggler. "I don't believe I've seen Carrie for a year at least. I've been up here, Margo and I have, for almost half a year. So I haven't seen Carrie for at least that long."

"Not even over the pixphone?"

"Pixphone rates from here to the planet are high, since it's a toll call," said Brian.

Jolson said, "Even so, you pixed her twice in the past month. Talked ten minutes on the first occasion, eleven on the second. Carrie phoned you three times. The last one was only two days before she was murdered."

He sank down further in his chair, sighing. "It wasn't the old romance starting up again, Jolson. I'd just as soon, though, that Margo didn't find out."

"What was going on?"

Moving his chair, Brian sat with his back to the juggling. "Carrie and I didn't break up just because of my behavior," he said, voice low. "See, I'd been getting these odd feelings about her. Carrie held an important position with Plaz, and my father's death . . . what do you know about that?"

"His skycar malfunctioned while he was traveling over Jungle #11. The car crashed and he was killed."

Holding up his left hand, Brian said, "Malfunction, they claimed. Except maybe it wasn't. From a few hints that Carrie had let drop . . . I don't know. I got the impression that some of those high-placed bastards at Plaz might have arranged his accident. Carrie included."

"Why?"

"I didn't have any idea," he said. "Not then, anyway."

"But Carrie got in touch with you again recently. She'd been feeling guilty and she wanted to talk to you."

"Something like that, yes, only Carrie wasn't that direct about it. You didn't know Carrie. She could never be direct," Brian said. "Teasing, hinting, that was her style."

"What did she imply?"

"That they were up to something at PlazHartz—still are for that matter. Carrie was involved; so was Dr. Windom. My father apparently opposed whatever it was they wanted to do."

"So they killed him."

"Yeah." He sighed again. "Probably I should've gone to the territorial police of the homicide squad. Told them to question Carrie and some of the others. But I felt I'd gotten away from all that, from his death and what happened to Jennifer—that's my sister. I didn't do anything, hoping I could just forget about it."

Jolson asked, "Have you seen your sister lately?"

"It makes me uneasy visiting her. Jennifer usually just sits there anyway, never speaks to me."

"You do call the Madhouse Spa."

"You obviously have gone over my pixphone bills," Brian said. "Yes, I call the damn place about once a week. Don't talk to her, just ask Dr. Ripperger how she's doing."

"You last phoned three days ago. What did he tell you?"

"Same as always. Jennifer's about the same. No improvement, probably never will be, but don't give up hope." He frowned, reached out to take hold of Jolson's arm. "Jennifer is okay, isn't she? Sometimes I get the feeling—"

"Far as I know," said Jolson, moving up and away from him. "I'll keep in touch with you."

Brian stood. "If you find out for sure that they did kill my father . . ." He let the sentence die, shaking his head slowly. "Hell, what difference would it make if you did tell me? I probably wouldn't do a goddamn thing."

"I'll tell you anyway," promised Jolson.

CHAPTER 14

Jolson came hurrying down the sun-drenched afternoon hillside. He was younger and smaller, not more than twenty-seven and hardly taller than five foot four. He was a human, sandy-haired and pink-cheeked, and wearing a two-piece medsuit of crisp white.

He leaped over a low picket fence, trotted along the gravel path and went bounding up the redbrix front steps of the main building of the Madhouse Spa complex. It was a three-story shingle building, bright white with green shutters.

He was three quick steps along the wide linoplaz front hallway when a large robot dog snarled at him.

The copper mechanical hound was stationed next to a groutfoot umbrella stand.

"Where the nurf you think you're going, pecker?" it inquired in a growly voice.

"Am I in time?" Jolson bent to make eye contact with the watchdog.

"In time for me to chomp a hunk out of your toke."

Straightening, Jolson spread his arms wide and grinned. "Don't you recognize me?"

"I don't have that sort of capability. You got to come

in, give the password of the day and continue on your way," explained the dog. "No password, I attack."

"Here I thought I was famous throughout the Hellquad System." Chuckling ruefully, Jolson knelt, suddenly slapped his left hand against the dog's neck.

"Yike." The robot's glaz eyes flared red, spun twice, clicked shut.

The small disabler he'd palmed was working. Pocketing it, Jolson continued upward. He was heading for the third level where, according to information provided by Dr. IQ, the head of the Madhouse Spa had his offices.

Halfway up a ramp he encountered a human nurse, a thin orange-haired woman.

"You're not supposed to be here, sir. At least I don't think so."

Grinning, he spread his arms wide. "Don't you recognize me? Dr. Floyd Christmas!"

"Well, you do look sort of familiar, Doctor. Can you give me another hint?"

"My dear woman, don't you possess a vidwall? Don't you read *Galactic Time-Life*?" he asked her, flapping his arms. "Dr. Floyd Christmas, the wonder boy of neoneutronics!"

"Oh, yes. You're the clever young fellow who installed a plastic brain in a gorilla last month on Fazenda. Though why exactly one would go to all that troub—"

"I certainly hope I'm in time to aid Dr. Ripperger."

"Aid him in what? The old boy's taking his afternoon snooze in his—"

"It's my understanding that I've been summoned here to assist in an emergency brain transplant, nurse."

"I hardly think so. We keep them under control with massive doses of drugs and a lot of electroshock," she told him. "I don't believe Dr. Ripperger's performed any surgery for years and years. Just as well, if you ask me, since he hits the old sauce pretty heavy these—"

"He wouldn't have summoned me if the situation wasn't urgent. I'll rush right up to his side." Smiling boyishly, he dodged around her to run on up the ramp.

Dr. Ripperger was an ample man of sixty, bewhiskered, clad in a three-piece medsuit and stretched out on his back on a floating tan davenport. He was snoring enthusiastically, hands folded over his rising and falling middle.

A dozen diplomas, attesting to degrees earned all over the universe, dotted the dark neowood walls of the large office. A near-empty plazflask of Château Discount port wine lay on its side near the foot of the davenport, along with one of the doctor's groutskin boots.

Rolling the psychotherapist's chair over to the slumbering man's side, Jolson straddled it. "Hi, Dr. Ripperger," he said in an enthusiastic voice, nudging him with a fist. "Hey, did I drop in at an inappropriate time?"

"Man the lifeboats! She's going to . . ." Ripperger sat up, stroked at his bristly white beard and focused his bleary gaze on his visitor. "What's the meaning of this intrusion, young man?"

"Don't tell me you don't recognize me either, Doctor." Jolson smiled. "Dr. Floyd Christmas."

"Ah, the upstart," said the head of the Madhouse Spa. "How'd you get up here? I keep an exceptionally mean-minded dog stationed in the lower hallway to savage just such arrogant mooncalves as—"

"I'm running on a pretty tight schedule," explained Jolson. "So we'd best get to the point."

"There is absolutely nothing I care to discuss with you, Dr. Christmas," Ripperger said. "I happened to read a piece of yours in *Expensive Vacations for Medical People Journal* on the alleged misuse of stunguns on disturbed patients. I read between the lines, as it were, and knew at once that you were slyly attacking me although you never so much as mentioned my—"

Whap!

Having extracted a small coin-sized coppery truthdisc from his pocket, Jolson slapped it against the doctor's neck. He was careful to make contact with flesh and not whiskers. "What you find stuck in you now is a fairly powerful and sophisticated truthdisc," he explained. "It was originally developed in the Barnum System for the exclusive use of crackerjack agents in the espionage line. From this moment on, Dr. Ripperger, you'll tell me exactly what I want to know."

"That's a lot of . . . No, by Jove, you turn out to be absolutely right, Christmas, my boy. I am compelled to sit here like a docile ninny."

"Furthermore, when I remove it, you'll drop off to sleep once more and awake sometime later with no notion of my visit."

"The devil you say." His eyes were now glazed in a new way and he sat stiffly, hands at his sides.

"Where is Jennifer Lenz?"

"Why, she's . . . confound it . . . she is not here."

"Where is she?"

"I don't know."

"Explain that."

"She was taken away."

"When?"

"Roughly two months ago."

"Who took her?"

The doctor was still struggling against the truth drug that was being pumped into him. "It . . . Jove, I do wish I didn't have to blurt . . . the girl was taken by minions of . . . of Dr. Heather Windom."

"Are you telling me Jennifer was kidnapped from here?"

"No, she was removed with my knowledge."

"Meaning you're in cahoots with Dr. Windom."

"She's had a controlling interest in this establishment for several years."

"Why did she want Jennifer out of here?"

"I honestly do not know."

"What do you think?"

"Heather is a very ambitious woman. She has many complex schemes afoot—schemes about which I know precious little. It is my assumption that Jennifer is to be utilized in connection with one of these plans."

"You have no idea where the girl is being held?"

"None whatsoever."

"Make a guess."

"I'd venture to say Jennifer is still on this planet. Heather has considerable business and real-estate holdings. The young woman could be at any of several locations."

"Tell me, in layman's terms, what's wrong with Jennifer."

"Not a blessed thing."

Jolson straightened up. "Then why was she here?"

"Heather's orders."

"But her brother says she suffered a breakdown."

"That was induced by drugs. Heather's idea."

"And Jennifer was kept that way?"

"Usually we didn't use anything on the child while she was being kept in our maximum-security holding complex. Perhaps you passed that on the way here—Honeysuckle Lodge? On any day when she had a visit from her brother or one of her few remaining friends, she was stupefied by drugs and electroshock."

"You're a vicious son of a bitch."

"Yes, and I've found it a most profitable profession, old man."

"How many other patients like Jennifer do you have here?"

"Twenty-two at the moment."

"On Dr. Windom's orders?"

"Not at all. I have many other customers."

"Why do this to Jennifer in the first place?"

"She was apparently suspicious about something. Rather than kill her, Heather sent her to me. Humane in a way, don't you know."

"What was she suspicious about?"

"It had to do with something her father stumbled upon shortly prior to his death. She was considered dangerous."

"Details?"

"I made it my business not to find out. That way Heather won't ever get the notion that I'm dangerous."

"Did Heather kill Simon Lenz?"

For nearly five seconds the doctor fought against answering. "Yes . . . she was the head of the group that planned it, arranged it."

"Why was he killed?"

"I don't know, except that he stood in the way of plans Heather had for PlazHartz."

"But Jennifer knows?"

"Some of it anyway."

Jolson said, "Android replicas of Simon Lenz. What do you know about them?"

"A project of Jennifer's, before she was brought here. She's really quite gifted a technician. Pity in a way she wasn't able to pursue that while here with us, but it couldn't be helped."

"Why'd she build them?"

"She wanted working models of a new superior type of android she'd designed. The young woman actually does have an exaggerated admiration for her father. She conceived the idea of making a half dozen replicas of Simon Lenz at different ages, from adolescence to maturity. She intended thereby to demonstrate to him her ability and also give him a sort of familial gift. He died before they were all completed."

"They're completed now?"

"So I believe."

"Where are they?"

"They were kept at the Lenz estate for a time."

"But now?"

"I honestly don't know the current whereabouts of the androids."

"They're being used to kill select employees of Plaz-Hartz."

"I know nothing of that."

"Is Heather using them?"

"I don't know."

Jolson paused for a moment. Then he pulled the truth-disc free of the doctor's neck.

Ripperger sank back, stretched out and resumed snoring.

"I'll be back to see about springing the rest of your alleged patients," promised Jolson.

CHAPTER 15

Dr. IQ gazed fondly around him. "Ar, I dearly love this place."

"That's to be expected," said Jolson.

"While you're pretending to be browsing with me, I'll pass along what new information I've dredged up."

Three walls of the shop were covered with rows of cubbyholes. Each compartment had a small seethru plaz door covering it, and each held a plyowrapped chunk of cheese.

"Before you get to that," Jolson said, "I have another new assignment for you."

IQ started along one wall, scanning the rows of cheese. Trailing him was a red robot shopping cart. "How's this Venusian bleu look to you?"

"It's got green fungus on it."

"Supposed to." Deciding against the bleu, the ratman moved on. "Cheddar's dull. So is Cheshire."

"Delve some more into Dr. Heather Windom's background," Jolson said. "I want to know about her assets, what companies she owns. Locations. I'm especially interested in any place where you could keep a young woman prisoner and also maybe store six androids."

"We're talking about a specific young lady?"

"Jennifer Lenz."

"Then she wasn't at the Madhouse Spa?"

"Nope, your information was right."

"Usually is. Here's a handsome troo cheese." He fingered a coin out of his overcoat pocket, clicked it into the slot beside the compartment. The lid flipped open and Dr. IQ lifted out the wrapped wedge of cheese.

"Okay, now, what did you find out about the guy Buster saw tampering with the Killdozer car last night?"

The ratman placed the wedge carefully in his cart and then continued his tour of the shop. "I don't care much for Gjetost, but maybe I'll pick up that new Gloucester. It comes from Barnum, your home planet."

"The attempt on my life?"

"The spindly birdman your robot thinks he saw is a fellow named Oscar Wilborn," said the ratman while going through the ritual required to acquire another hunk of cheese. "Wilborn most often teams with a dogman known as Murdstone Slim. Slim's specialty is rigging parasite controls on landcars. He's been involved in at least sixty murders since arriving in our system some five years back. You were lucky that pretty young woman came along to—"

"Where do I find this pair?"

"You may not have to," said Dr. IQ. "I don't rely entirely on computers. The pixphone can also work wonders when used judiciously and with some finesse."

"You found out who they're working for?"

"Exactly. It happens to be a private eye—a lot of them cluttering up this case, did you notice?—name of Van Trocadero. A humanoid with offices over in Safe Zone #16. He does not have a sterling reputation."

"Who's his client?"

"As yet I do not know," admitted IQ. "Perhaps, if you pay him a call, you can find that out for yourself and spare me additional effort."

"Perhaps."

A warm rain began to fall as twilight took over the streets. The private investigator Jolson sought had his office in a penthouse suite in a seven-story building that overlooked a small neglected square. The big raindrops splattered on the plazstone path that cut through the overgrown grass of the square, hit at the knee-high purplish grass and splashed Jolson's fur.

He turned up the collar of his cloak, brushed at his plump furry face. He had once again assumed the identity of Pud Humazoo, Jr., the rakehell catman.

"Buy a bunch of meech flowers?" queried a frail grey-feathered birdwoman who was stationed to the right of the entrance to Trocadero's building. "Wear them in your buttonhole, gift a loved one, place them on a grave."

"Do go away, old girl," drawled Jolson as the glaz lobby doors whooshed open in anticipation of his entering.

"Only twenty trubux, and the buggers smell absolutely gorgeous."

"They are not one half as fragrant as you, dear lady."

"Hell, it's my last bunch. Take 'em as a gift." Tossing the pinkish flowers to him, she started away into the rain.

Jolson held the flowers in his paw as he started across the neovinyl floor of the oval lobby.

He happened to poke a furry finger into the bouquet. "Whoa now." Pivoting, he ran back the way he'd come.

The doors whispered open for him and Jolson dived out into the rainy dusk.

The fragile flower vendor was nowhere in sight.

Disabling the listening bug he'd discovered in the meech flowers, Jolson dropped it in his pocket. It was not the same type as those he'd found planted on him earlier.

The flowers he deposited in a dispozhole near the elevators.

"Instead of bland, mindless music while in transit," explained the voxbox in the ceiling of his cage, "we're experimenting with more uplifting and stimulating fare. Here then, as part of our brand-new Masterpiece Elevator Rides series, is Professor W. R. Truett, respected authority on Earth literature. His topic for this initial lecture is 'Meaning and Nonmeaning in the Early Mass-Market Paperback Novels of Harlan Ellison.' Please to begin, Prof . . ."

The door opened and Jolson stepped out on the seventh level, leaving the lecture behind.

There was no reception room. The door opened directly on Van Trocadero's private office. He was a broad-shouldered blond humanoid of forty-some years, seated behind a cast-iron desk and smoking the same kind of foul cigar Lou Killdozer favored. "Mr. Humazoo, is it? I've been expecting you."

"I'm obliged to tell you, old sock," began Jolson as he, uninvited, lowered his bulk into the rubberoid client chair, "that thus far I am not impressed. I was accosted by a feathery old crone on your very doorstep, as it were, and—"

"Listen, Humazoo, you have to expect that in this district. The rent, though, more than—"

"This particular old wretch attempted to plant what I believe is called in your trade a bug upon my person."

Trocadero's cigar fell completely free of his mouth as he sat upright. "Holy mackerel! Not another one."

"How's that?"

"Nothing, nothing. I suffer from a very mild, benign almost, nervous disorder that causes me to blurt out meaningless phrases from time to time," said Trocadero. "It in no way affects my abilities as a shamus." Noticing that the fallen cigar was smoldering in his out basket, he retrieved it.

"Others have tried to sneak listening devices into your lair, old sock?"

"No, nothing like that."

"Might I next ask if you've checked this office itself for bugs lately?"

"Sixteen minutes ago," answered the hefty detective. "Not that it needed it especially, more for practice really."

"How many did you find, though?"

"Three . . . um . . . that is to say, none."

Jolson edged his chair closer to the black desk. "The case I wish to consult you on, Mr. Trocadero, is a most delicate one," he confided. "As I hinted on the pixphone, it's a situation that must be kept confidential, involving as it does threats of breach-of-promise suits, charges of reckless tattooing."

"Discretion is our specialty."

"I am reluctant to unburden myself if there are eavesdropping gadgets drinking in my every—"

"This office is absolutely bug-free. Trust me."

"You're certain?"

"Completely."

"Good." Jolson rose in his chair, reached out and slapped the truthdisc against the detective's neck.

"What kind of flim . . ." He leaned to his left, eyes blinking and cigar falling once again.

"You're going to answer all my questions truthfully."

"I will, yes."

"Last night you hired two gents—Wilborn and Murdstone Slim—to arrange for the death of Lou Killdozer."

"I did . . . but listen . . . we shouldn't be talking about this . . ." Trocadero's hands were clutching the arms of his chair.

"Who's your client on this one?"

"I'm not supposed to . . . God, if I . . ."

"C'mon, you have to tell me."

"You don't understand . . . I have a PlazHartz heart . . . special additions in mine that I didn't know about when it was put in . . . I have to do what she . . . but it's rigged so I can't talk . . . if I do . . ."

"What sort of dodge is this?"

"It's rigged to—" He shot to his feet, both hands sweeping up to clutch at his chest.

Something inside his chest commenced making a harsh keening sound. Next came loud brittle chattering and a mounting droning hum.

Leaving his chair, Jolson threw himself toward the wall.

An instant later Trocadero's plaz heart exploded, blowing the front of him away.

CHAPTER 16

Jolson was watching the heavy rain fall on the villa grounds. Turning away from the window, he resumed pacing.

When he passed the mantel, he asked the voxclock, "Time?"

"Six minutes later than it was when you last inquired, sir."

Nodding, he returned to the window.

There was Molly's crimson landcar returning.

Jolson left the house to meet her. "I expected you earlier."

"So did I." She slid out of the car, long legs first. "Certain aspects of the operative's life can be darn discomforting, Ben."

"What's that spot on your dress?"

"Most likely a fingerprint."

"You saw a PlazHartz executive?"

Molly took his arm and they entered the rented villa together. "A gentleman named Ozzie Washborg, yes. A yellow-haired human, quite taken with me."

"He's on the list."

Letting go of him, Molly walked over to the sofa and

sat, legs going wide. "If he wasn't, I wouldn't have devoted what seemed like several days of my life to him this afternoon." She brushed at a tangle of red hair. "We had a preliminary meeting, followed by a lengthy business discussion, followed by cocktails. By cocktails he was using both hands."

Jolson said, "I started to worry an hour ago."

She smiled faintly up at him. "That's thoughtful."

"Did you manage to set up a dinner date?"

"Would've been impossible not to," replied Molly. "I'm meeting him in two hours at the *Bayside Queen,* a houseboat restaurant about two miles up the shore from here. Supposed to be very private."

"A good place to have a quiet conversation with Washborg."

"You'll have to approach him at or before the soup course, Ben, because I don't guarantee how long I can refrain from slugging him." She swung her legs up onto the sofa. "And how was your day?"

"Nobody fell in love with me, although a robot dog seriously considered biting me."

"What did you learn?"

He lifted her legs, sat on the sofa and arranged them across his lap. "I'll tell you," he said, and did.

"His heart blew up?" She took her legs back and sat up as he concluded his report.

"Yep. It was a PlazHartz heart, Model EX/104P."

"How do you know . . . oh. There was enough left for you to tell."

"This rival private eye had to be working for Dr. Heather Windom."

"Working against his will. Isn't that what the guy was trying to tell you?"

"Looks like they can rig those hearts, certain ones anyway, to control people," said Jolson. "This particular model is a fairly expensive one."

"Meaning richer, more important people have them installed."

"Right now on this planet alone there are sixty-six thousand citizens walking around with that particular model inside them."

She shivered. "That's appalling and . . . um . . . insidious."

"At the very least."

"Now, don't make fun of me," said Molly. "It's just that I'm not used to uncovering plots of this magnitude."

"We're not sure of the magnitude yet," he reminded.

"Seems obvious to me. Dr. Windom and probably most of the folks on that list cooked up a plan to use PlazHartz implants to control important people in government, industry, show business and who knows what else on Farpa." She stood up. "But why stop with this planet? These hearts are used all over the Hellquad System and they've been branching out to our system as well."

"We'll have to stop them."

Molly said, "It seems like somebody else is trying to stop them already. Using the Simon Lenz androids."

"And who might that be?"

"Well, it has to be Jennifer Lenz, the daughter. We know she had a morbid crush on her father and—" Molly fisted her left hand and hit her thigh. "Heck, none of that is actually true, is it? That was just propaganda set up by Dr. Windom."

"Jennifer's more than likely a patsy for something."

"They want her blamed for the killings. Except I'm still not exactly certain who they are," she said. "Well, I'd

better change for my dinner date. Into something that
won't show paw marks." She kissed him on the cheek.
"Thanks for being concerned."

"You're welcome." He kissed her on the cheek.

"I hope der chentleman vill eggscuse der dod-busted
interruption," said Jolson, intruding once more into the
private dining room on the upper deck of the moored
Bayside Queen.

"What is it now?" Ozzie Washborg was a thick blond
man of forty, wearing a three-piece purple funsuit. He had
an arm around Molly's shoulders.

Molly pushed him away and moved around to the oppo-
site side of the small floating table, dragging her chair
along. "I'm glad you dropped in, waiter," she said,
smoothing her dress.

"Chass? Und how might I be uff service, dear lady?" He
was plump and green, an exact replica, down to the authentic accent, of a typical Venusian waiter.

"Well, I think I'd like to peruse the list of Earth wines."

"Der lady got svell taste, begauze dem vines is der best
dod-gozzled vines in der whole—"

"Honey, don't you think domestic wine'd be fine?"

"Certainly, Oz, if you think you can't afford—"

"It isn't a question of afford, honey," the PlazHartz vice
president told her. "I'm just getting damn tired of this
emerald oaf's barging in here every other minute, and if
he has to go fetch another wine list and then come back
again—"

"Ah, but dot's vhere der chentleman is wrong." Jolson
touched a sausagelike green finger to his green dumpling
of a nose. "Chust a minute." Waddling, he went to the
private room's full-length window, which was giving a

view of the rainswept deck and the dark bay beyond. He flicked a toggle, and the window went black.

"What's the idea of getting rid of the damn view?" Washborg wanted to know. "I like a dash of scenery until I'm ready to move into the more private phases of—"

"Vot you don't know yet is vot ve got in mind for you," said Jolson cordially as he approached him. "Led me oxplain." He smiled and slapped a truthdisc to Washborg's neck.

"Is this some kind of . . ." He took on a blank expression.

"Go easy, Ben," cautioned Molly. "In case he's got the same sort of heart as the private eye."

Jolson had already undone the front of Washborg's tunic. "Nope, no sign he's had any kind of transplant at all."

"Mr. Washborg, you'll have to answer each and every question we ask," Molly told the drugged man.

"Sure, honey."

Jolson asked, "How do you control people with the PlazHartz heart?"

"Heather came up with that idea originally. It's really quite simple to modify the heart so it pumps a mind-controlling drug into the bloodstream and up to the old brain."

"How many people have you done this to thus far?"

"Since we began the program two years ago we've enlisted—that's what Heather likes to call it—we've enlisted seventy-six hundred key figures on Farpa. We planted seventeen modified hearts this week alone. That adds to our list of controlled individuals the Lord Mayor of Sunspa 3, the second vice president of the Hydroponic Farmers Bank, the quizmaster of *Toad for a Day* and a whole stewpot of others. Some weeks, like this one, we're lucky and a nice bunch of usable people sign up for the transplants. And since we have several prominent surgeons on our side, we can also persuade officials and personalities we're interested in to have their hearts replaced with ours even when they don't actually need a new one."

"But Simon Lenz opposed the idea?"

"He lacked vision, as Heather put it," said the mind-controlled Washborg. "Why, in the past two years, thanks to all the opportunities this has added, we grossed over two billion trudollars extra. You divide that into thirteen shares and . . . well, only nine shares now."

"Who's killing your cohorts?"

"I don't know. It's got me scared."

"What about Jennifer Lenz?"

"I thought maybe she could be behind it, except she's locked away at some loony bin."

"What—"

Jolson never got the opportunity to finish the question.

The entire wide window all at once shattered and fell away.

A lean redheaded young man, freckled and not more than sixteen, leaped into the room from the rain-slick deck. He held a silvery kilgun in his left hand.

CHAPTER 17

Rain came slashing into the room as the freckled intruder aimed his kilgun at Ozzie Washborg. "You killed Simon Lenz!"

Jolson's bulky green body hopped to the left and he kicked out at the table, slamming it into the stupefied target.

Washborg teetered, falling sideways off his chair toward the floor.

Molly, meantime, had flipped free of her chair and gone rolling toward the nearest wall. She reached under her glossy sinsilk skirt for her thigh holster.

The youthful assassin fired his kilgun in the direction of the toppling man.

Zzzzzzitzzzzz!

The crackling greenish beam missed by nearly a yard, digging a saucer-sized hole in both carpeting and floor.

Jolson drew his disabler pistol from the pocket of his tuxsuit. He fired at the Lenz android.

Zzzzzaccccckkkkk!

That didn't bother the red-haired youth at all. Spreading his legs wide, he prepared to take another shot at the sprawled PlazHartz vice president.

Molly took a shot at the android with her stungun.

Zzzzzzummmmmmm!

The beam hit him in the side, causing him to sway and take a staggering step to the right.

Zzzzzzitttzzzzzz!

He got off a second shot, but it went wide and sliced the table in half.

Spinning on his heel, the android ran out onto the rainy deck and vaulted deftly over the railing.

"Retrieve the truthdisc and follow me," Jolson called to Molly as he sprinted across the room, crunching fragments of window glaz underfoot. "We'll have to abandon Ozzie for now."

The rain came rushing down at him, hitting hard at his plump green body. He reached the rail in time the see the andy go scurrying out along a dock down below and jump into a waiting waterlaunch.

Jolson climbed backwards over the railing, dropped to the gritty ground ten feet below.

Unused to jumping around in his present form, he didn't land as well as he might have. He hit on his hip and knee, slid along the rough wet ground. As he pushed upright and started for the small pier a hundred yards away, the launch was already moving away from him into the rainswept night bay.

Moored at the rickety pier's end was a small tourbarge. Its open deck was ringed with benches and covered over with a fringed awning. A flickering glosign leaning against the gangplank announced FARPA HISTORICAL SOCIETY BAY TOURS.

A frogman in a three-piece blue funsuit occupied a neocanvas chair at the foot of the gangway. "Our next scenic and highly enlightening excursion around the lovely waters of the bay doesn't commence for approximately another forty minutes, gov," he said, holding up a roll of faxtickets. "You may wish, however, to purchase your ducats now so as to avoid the anticipated rush. Since all sorts of extra activities are scheduled for the bay this—"

"We're sailing right now." Jolson took out a hundred-trudollar bill, tossed it to the frogman.

"I fear, gov, you didn't grasp my earlier comments about our schedule for this even—"

"Now." Jolson produced a stungun.

"As you say. Embark right away and have a jolly sail, I'm sure." Leaving his chair while folding up the money, he moved several feet along the pier.

"Hey, how much did you slip him?" Molly was hobbling along the rain-slick planking. "We can't afford to keep spending money as though—"

"Get aboard," urged Jolson.

She obliged, limping up the gangplank after him. "Boy, am I disappointed. I'm wearing an antigrav belt under this dress—which also spoils the hang of it—and yet when I leaped off the darn houseboat I plummeted like a lodestone. When you pay a hundred and seventy-six thousand trudollars for—"

"Lodestones don't plummet."

Jolson hurried across the empty deck to the controls of the barge. After scanning the setup for a few seconds, he got the boat going and guided it free of the pier.

There came a large cracking noise.

"You probably should've unhooked that gangplank before we took off," mentioned Molly. "Not that I know all that much about things nautical, but—"

"That green light way up ahead—the one that's receding very rapidly—is on the tail end of our android's launch. Keep him in sight if you can."

Molly rested her bare elbows on the wet rail. "How come your disabler didn't faze him, and my stungun hardly at all?"

"He's supposed to be a special kind of android," he reminded. "Something new that Jennifer came up with."

"We are now fast approaching, ladies and gentlemen, the justly renowned Old Polluted Beachfront," began a voxbox attached to the frets of the awning. "It was on this historic site just ninety years ago that—"

Zzzzzacccckkkkk!

The box ceased lecturing as Jolson put away his disabler pistol.

"Ben, I don't see his light any longer."

"Think he just swung into that brightly lit area up ahead."

"Appears to be some sort of celebration going on, all sorts of people milling around and—look there—fireworks," she said. "Seems like an odd place for a killer to be holing up."

There were nearly a hundred soggy people on the wide stone dock, most of them silent, watching hopefully as the still-green Jolson and the slightly limping Molly climbed up the slippery stone steps from where they'd moored the borrowed barge.

The expectant group included a brass band made up of twenty-six catmen in scarlet-and-gold unisuits, several assorted food vendors, a restless group of young men standing, shuffle-footed, beneath a banner identifying them as the Preacher O'Brien School for Homeless Hooligans

Boys' Choir and a scatter of birdmen and catmen in tux-suits and colored glosashes.

"I knew the fireworks would start attracting folks," said the jovial catman who trotted over and held out a welcoming paw. "Glad to have you with us to celebrate the fiftieth anniversary of the Spirit of Purity Statue."

Hugging herself and wrapping the section of plyotarp she'd brought from the barge tighter around her shoulders, Molly observed, "I don't notice any statue."

"What'd I tell you, Vernon?" A lean tuxsuited birdman joined them. "I told you there being no statue would cause tourists to—"

"Earl, we got all the ceramic replicas of the statue over there in the souvenir booths, we got loaves of bread shaped like the statue, we got a cake three and one half feet high that looks as much like it as a cake can look like a forty-foot-high statue depicting—"

"What we haven't got is the statue." Earl pointed a feathery finger at the empty pedestal that rose up behind the small watchful crowd. "Hooligans made off with it under the cover of darkness two nights back, but the selectman here insisted we—"

"Hey, we never stole your lousy statue," protested one of the choirboys, spitting.

"Yeah, that's a bum rap."

"Anyways, we got alibis."

"I didn't mean *Homeless* Hooligans, lads," explained the birdman. "I apologize, however, for my unfortunate use of words."

Jolson told the jovial selectman, "Actually we've been looking forward to this fete for weeks. My dear wife especially has—"

"I keep a ceramic copy of the Spirit of Purity on the

mantel," Molly informed them. "Right next to my snerg."

"The thing is," said Jolson, rubbing at his round green nose, "we were supposed to meet my wife's cousin here. His launch is anchored down below, yet—"

"Red-haired lad?" asked Earl. "Mite on the wide-eyed and surly side?"

"That's Simon to the life," said Molly. "Is he here?"

"We invited him to stick around," said the catman, "but he hurried on."

"Did you notice which way he went?" asked Jolson.

Both officials pointed to the twisting street that led away from the dock.

"He rushed off along Bay Street there," Earl told them. "I have to tell you good people that he didn't look like he was in the mood for much celebrating. But then, few people do seem to be this evening. What with torrential rains and the lack of a statue."

"Now, Earl, there's no call to keep looking on the—"

"Much obliged for your help," said Jolson. "We'll find him and drag him back."

"You wouldn't care to watch a few folk dances before you go?" asked the catman, without much hope.

"When we return that'll be the first thing we'll want to see," promised Jolson, guiding Molly in the wake of the android.

CHAPTER 18

Molly was wearing the plyotarp over her head and shoulders now like a hooded cloak. "Maybe I should've slipped the selectman our card," she said as they trudged along the wet plazstone street. "Finding a missing statue ought to be fairly easy, compared with locating a murderous andy in this maze of gloomy buildings."

"Harder to hide a forty-foot-high statue," agreed Jolson. "Don't glance, but there's somebody lurking in that shadowy doorway across the street."

"Is it the android?"

Jolson slowed. "Nope, it— Damn, it's Buster."

"Buster the robot who's Lou Killdozer's driver and bodyguard?"

"That Buster, yes." He tugged her into a dim alley they were passing and halted. "We'd best go have a chat with him."

"I'm standing in something that feels like a bunch of dead fish." She bent and squinted. "That's exactly what it is."

"Let's go talk to Buster."

Molly's tarp crackled as she turned to stare at him. "You're your Jolson self again."

"No use confusing him." Slipping an arm through hers, he escorted her across the rainy roadway. "Hey, Buster, what are you doing hereabouts?"

The robot's head emerged a bit from the turned-up collar of his plaid overcoat. "Jolson, is that youse?"

"None other."

"Youse better slip me the password, just to be on the safe—"

"Chameleon."

"I got to tell you, this caper's turning sort of screwy," Buster confided. "See, I been tailing Sally, just like I was instructed."

"Is she around here?"

"In that warehouse down the corner. The one says HyperProduce on its front."

"What's perplexing you?"

"I could of swore I seen Lou leaving that dump about two hours ago. Except he's supposed to be dead and done for."

"Oh, so?"

"Yeah, and he didn't look exactly right. He had long blond pansy hair, plus a beard, and he wasn't dressed with his usual flair," said the robot. "Matter of fact, Jolson, I also don't think much of them rags you're sporting. Too conservative and a few sizes too big."

"Did you follow the guy with the golden locks?"

"Naw, because youse told me to watch the old lady. And she's still in that dump yonder."

"And the lad hasn't come back yet?"

"Not yet, so I— Well, how about that? There he is now, sneaking along close to that brix wall over there."

Across the rainswept street a thickset blond man was

furtively hurrying. He wore a heavy dark overcoat, carried a dark case tucked under his arm.

"That is Lou Killdozer," whispered Molly, "with false whiskers and a wig."

"Toting a vidcam case," added Jolson. "Buster, how long has Sally been here?"

"About three hours this time," the robot replied. "But she's visited it a couple times since I began tailing her. I would of reported that to youse except youse never contacted me like youse promised."

Jolson said, "I'll take a look around inside that joint." He patted Molly on the shoulder. "You stick here."

"Oughtn't I to—"

"If I don't return in a reasonable time, do something drastic." He went running through the hard rain.

Judging by the smells in the big dark room, Jolson had stepped into an immense salad. He adjusted his eyes and scanned the warehouse. Neowood crates of vegetables were stacked in neat rows all around—purple lettuce spacejumped in from Murdstone, blue carrots from Fazenda, square tomatoes from Earth.

At first he heard only the drumming of the rain on the arched roof. Gradually he became aware of voices.

Quietly he walked along a dark aisle between crates. At the far end of the big room a thin line of light showed at floor level.

Jolson eased closer to that door, listening.

". . . acting like a walleyed gump," the voice of Strangler Sally Killdozer was accusing.

"C'mon, Ma, quit bitching at me," complained Lou.

"You were supposed to tail those damn andies the next

time one went prowling," she said. "Get us vidpix—real proof—of him knocking off somebody."

"Listen, Ma, it ain't my fault he decided to use a hot-damn boat," said her son. "I tracked him to the docks, but then—"

"Fourteen years an op and you couldn't steal a boat for yourself and take off after him?"

"There was hundreds of guys in fancy costumes and band uniforms hanging around that part of the waterfront. There was even forty or so runty kids with songbooks in their mitts," explained the unhappy private investigator. "I'm telling you, on the level, I couldn't swipe a boat. There was one a little ways off that looked like a possibility, but as I was heading for it they started shooting off fireworks and—"

"Okay, let's look on the goddamn bright side. What do we have?"

"I got some swell new footage of the redheaded andy leaving the ServoBot factory over on Front Street," said Lou. "The shots of him returning ain't bad either."

"He must've gone out to knock off another PlazHartz muckamuck tonight, Lou. If we had pictures of that, then we could hit Dr. Windom," said Sally. "We'd have a real stranglehold on that skinny broad. Furthermore, we could stop her from trying to knock you off."

"We maybe got enough on her already, Ma. We know they're using them Simon Lenz androids to kill off the partners they don't need anymore," said Lou, puffing on his cigar. "I also got a vidtape of my prelim talk with Carrie Tinsley. That's where the bimbo tells me about the overall plan, the control of important ginks with them special PlazHartz hearts."

"But Dr. Windom's wise to you. She warned you and

then she tried to bump you off," reminded his mother.
"Yeah, and look what happened to that Tinsley broad.
They got you on their shit list now, too."

"So what? They'll kill that sap Jolson if they kill anybody."

"If they can find the lop-eared bastard. I ain't laid eyes
on him nor Buster for a whole and entire day," she said.
"Lieutenant Fairball's been chewing my toke because Jolson was supposed to go in and talk to him."

Jolson, nodding thoughtfully to himself, took his leave.

CHAPTER 19

Putting his needle and thread aside, the black man left his stool near the cash register and ambled over to their booth. "You're probably thinking," he said as he adjusted his grey wig and smoothed his lace-trimmed apron, "that this is a poor location for a tea shoppe."

Jolson turned away from the window that gave him a view of Front Street outside. "You have to admit Mother Malley's Cozy Tea Shoppe isn't exactly a waterfront dive."

"That's what I keep telling them." The proprietor straightened the doily under the dainty table lamp. "But you can't fight their marketing strategy. See, Mother Malley is a chain operation and they're determined to have a tea shoppe every three square miles in this territory."

Molly closed her menu. "I'll have a cup of Venusian Zinger tea."

Fetching an order pad out of his lace-trimmed apron pocket, he wrote that down. "Another thing that's rough, they insist you have to wear the Mother Malley costume," he said. "You can well imagine the teasing I have to put up with from some of these unsavory dockwallopers."

"You ought to complain," suggested Jolson. "I'll have the Earthmint tea."

"Oh, I marched into corporate headquarters to lodge a protest, but when I met the board of directors and they were all sitting there with wigs and aprons, I knew I was destined to taste defeat." He returned to the kitchen of the small, nearly empty shop.

Molly nodded toward the wide brix building across the way. "The androids are stored in that ServoBot factory?"

"According to the conversation Lou had with his mom."

Molly whapped the table with her fist. "I'm darn miffed," she proclaimed. "Here that cigar-puffing lout has been alive all along. I was blubbering like a wee child over what I thought were his last remains. I even hyperwired flowers to Sally. That costs two hundred fifty-six trudollars, you know."

"They needed a decoy." He thumbed his chest. "After Lou talked to O'Brine, he happened to get together with Carrie Tinsley while he was poking around into the murder business. She was in need of extra funds and decided to tell him about the larger plot. Obviously they were figuring to blackmail Dr. Windom."

"Except she got wise," said Molly. "Lou, brilliant mind that he is, got a smart idea right after she had those goons warn him to lay off. He knew BIDS employs several ex-Chameleons."

"Right, so they flimflammed you into sending me out here to play Lou Killdozer. He keeps on investigating, disguised with a wig and false whiskers, and I play target."

"Boy, and we own a controlling interest in their whole cheesy operation. That sure as heck isn't going to do our reputation throughout the universe any good."

"From what I overheard, the death of Carrie Tinsley hasn't disuaded the Killdozers."

"Well, we've got to clean up this mess first. Bring all the crooks to justice, put a stop to any and all—"

The bell over the door tinkled and a water-soaked birdman came in out of the rain. "Business awful as usual, eh, Leon?"

"Nope, I'd actually say it's picked up a touch, Earl." The proprietor set aside his embroidery.

"You think running a waterfront tea shoppe is a rough go, you ought to try staging a fair to commemorate the fiftieth darn anniversary of the Spirit of Purity statuette when you don't have the dang statue."

"Still missing, is it?"

"If you ask me, those choirboys made off with— Why, hello there, ma'am. Haven't found your cousin, eh?" The official came up to their booth.

Molly smiled ruefully. "I haven't, no," she answered. "And on top of that, as you may've noticed, I seem to have misplaced my husband."

"So I see. Wellsir, it's one of those nights."

"This kind gentleman has offered to aid me in my quest."

"Be careful you don't get jumped by hooligans," warned Earl before shuffling off to a booth of his own.

Jolson was watching the factory. "Somebody just came out."

"That's Joshua Larchmont," Molly said. "I met him at the PlazHartz offices."

"He's on the list, too." Jolson slid free of the booth. "I'll become him for a spell and get inside. You await me here."

"You're not in the same sort of clothes he—"

"I will be," he said, heading for the door, "once I catch up with Joshua."

The robot night watchman was seven feet high and had a glaring flashbeam built into his broad chest. He played the light over Jolson, blocking his entrance into the Servo-Bot building. "What now, Mr. Larchmont?"

"I left some important documents behind, my good man." Jolson was now a middle-sized human with ginger whiskers, decked out in a three-piece polka-dot cazsuit.

"I see your stammer's better, sir."

"C-c-comes and goes." Jolson had only heard Larchmont grunt. That was when the stungun beam had hit him and he'd toppled over in the alley a block and a half from here. Not much to build a voice on.

"Go on in, sir." The robot stepped aside.

Jolson crossed the threshold as the plaz doors whisked out of his way.

He was in a showroom that was lit with a scatter of light globes floating up near the eggshell-white ceiling. A dozen low pedestals ringed the room and on each stood a demo model robot or android.

There was a four-armed cleaning woman andy, a drink-mixing barbot, a very regal valet, a lovely blonde young woman in black neoleather holding a coiled whip.

"Something for everybody," murmured Jolson, heading for a ramp that led to the next level up.

On the next floor were rows of robots and androids, standing like a silent army. Butlers, barbots, houseboys, companions, watchmen.

No red-haired replicas of Simon Lenz, though.

He started up another ramp.

"Mr. Larchmont. Mr. Larchmont." A voxbox in the ceiling overhead started paging him.

After hesitating a second, Jolson called out, "W-w-what is it?"

"Important pixphone call. Take it in the nearest alcove, sir."

"Very well."

A few yards ahead the curved walls of a phone alcove commenced glowing.

Jolson entered it. "Yes?"

On the screen appeared a thin blonde woman of about forty. "Yes, I assumed you'd still be there, Josh."

It was Dr. Windom. "J-j-just leaving, Heather."

"I think not," she said with a thin smile. "After our earlier discussion this evening, I've decided that you, too, are deadwood."

"You can't—"

"Good-bye, darling." The phone screen blacked.

From the shadows at the upper end of the ramp a voice said, "You killed Simon Lenz."

CHAPTER 20

Jolson thrust his right hand into the side pocket of his newly acquired polka-dot jacket, yanked out the kilgun that had come with it and fired at the red-haired android that had just stepped into view with a kilgun of his own.

Zzzzzzittttttzzzzzzz!

This one was Simon Lenz at approximately thirty-five. The beam hit him smack in the forehead. It failed to penetrate, but the mechanical man was knocked off balance. He took three staggering steps to his left, hit the wall, dropped the silvery kilgun from his left hand.

Jolson meanwhile was galloping down the ramp. He hit the next level and went running along between the rows of servos. He hunched out of his jacket, tossed it into a floor dispozhole. Then he placed himself at the end of a row of butlers. He changed, taking on an aristocratic sneer and dark, slicked-down hair. He kept his new kilgun at his side and breathed as shallowly as possible.

"How bright is this fellow?" he asked himself. "Will he go by the face and overlook the polka-dot pants?"

If he had had time Jolson might have been able to swipe a butler outfit off one of the androids, ditch the thing and take its place. Lacking time, he had to hope.

"You killed Simon Lenz." The redheaded android was at the other end of the room.

Jolson could hear the rain hitting against the blind walls. He could hear, too, the slow, careful footfalls of the prowling android.

"You're going to die for what you did." The andy halted, was scanning a row of cleaning women. The kilgun was held up near his red head, pointing at the far-off ceiling.

He suddenly spun, swung the kilgun down and fired at a barbot.

Zzzzzzzitttttzzzzz!

The beam bored clean through the coppery chest. Gears, twists of wire, fragments of glaz tubes came spewing out the back of the servo. Smoke spilled out and then the robot tottered, lurched, fell.

"I'll find you eventually, Larchmont."

Jolson thought about that. He then concentrated for a moment and his face and person changed once more.

There was no guarantee the android wouldn't eventually shoot him merely by chance. Better not to continue being a butler.

"You killed Simon Lenz," Jolson said in a voice close to that of the android. Only it was younger, matching his twenty-year-old red-haired, freckled looks.

He left the row, went striding toward the android.

The andy frowned, letting his gun hand drop. "This is my assignment." He gave a negative shake of his head. "You weren't supposed to be activated."

"It's you who're here by mistake." Jolson stopped ten feet from the Simon Lenz dupe. "Get back to the storage area at once and allow me to dispose of Joshua Larchmont."

The elder Simon Lenz shook his head again. "No, this happens to be my kill," he insisted. "You have to clear out so— Ah! Polka-dot pants."

"How's that again?" Jolson took a few steps to his right, put himself closer to the row of cleaning ladies.

"I'm not wearing polka-dot pants."

"A shame, since they're all the rage this season." Three more steps to the right.

"Joshua Larchmont is wearing polka-dot pants."

"Proving my point about how fashionable they are."

"You may be Larchmont."

"Is that logical? I don't look at all like him," Jolson pointed out. "No, I look like you."

"It must be some sort of trick." The kilgun was pointing at Jolson.

"Let me remind you of a basic law of robotics," he said. "One mechanical man can't destroy another."

The android laughed. "I'm not a mechanical man. I'm Simon Lenz."

Another of Jennifer's touches.

"That's really quite an interesting philosophical stand." Jolson ducked behind a cleaning lady, shoved.

The four-armed scrubwoman rolled toward the killer android.

Zzzzzitttzzzzzz!

As the kilgun beam ripped through the cleaning lady's middle, Jolson dived behind another android. He pushed it hard, sending it forward and causing several more of the multiarmed servos to domino into each other and topple, collide and clank. There was considerable noise and confusion.

Jolson was crouched low, bicycling backwards and getting a line of barbots between him and the Simon Lenz simulacrum. He fired upward at the nearest floating light globe.

Zzzzzittttzzzzz!

The globe ceased to be and the room grew dimmer.

"I can see in the dark, Larchmont," called the android.

Jolson kicked a barbot, booting it into a blonde companion. Both crashed over, clanging and rattling.

All at once several servos fell over near the streetside wall.

And Molly was standing in the room, a bit dusty after having walked in through the thick wall. She held a mean-looking kilzooka nestled in her arms. "Ben, are you in here?"

He returned to his own persona. "Over here, but watch out," he said. "A kilgun won't stop him."

"Well, I just paid Mother Malley eleven thousand trudollars for this thing," she said, aiming it at the perplexed redheaded android. "He keeps it behind the stove to scare off rowdies." She turned the long, fat barrel on Simon Lenz. "Let's see if it works at all."

Kachow! Kachow!

The android's entire torso was ripped away, torn into twists of alloy and tatters of neocloth. The red-haired head seemed to float on nothing for a second and then it fell to the floor, bounced twice and rolled into the remains of the barbot. The legs doubled up, knelt, splayed and hit the floor one after the other.

Jolson steeplechased over the fallen android and reached Molly. "Thanks."

"I seem to be getting darn good at saving you from dire—"

"Can we both ride that wallwalker?"

"I don't see why not. As I understand the instruction

vidcaz that came with it, I can carry up to a thousand pounds of—"

"I suggest we exit."

"Don't we want to investigate further into the—"

"There are, I think, five more Simon Lenz andies to contend with," he told her. "And Dr. Windom may send in more troops of her own if she doesn't get a report back soon."

"Was that android trying to do you in?"

"Under the impression I was Larchmont."

Molly reached into her blouse. "I'll fiddle with the dials so we can both go out through the wall," she said, biting her lower lip as she concentrated. "Oh, and I better not forget to set the anti-gravity belt for the added weight. It was working okay, for a change, when I floated up to this level. I figured to start my own investigation on a floor other than the ground floor, because—"

"Tell me all that after we depart."

"Okay, Ben, put your arms around me. This should work."

He complied. A sharp pain zigzagged through his head, and then he felt as though he were undertaking a slow, sideways elevator ride.

"What do you know?" Molly gave a pleased laugh. "We did it."

They were standing on the wet night street. "Thanks again."

"I guess you can take your arms away from around me now," Molly suggested.

Joshua Larchmont fluffed his ginger whiskers, scowling mildly. "Why should I t-t-trust a chap who, by his own admission, s-s-stungunned me on a p-p-public thoroughfare and then d-d-dragged me to this rather p-p-pretentious villa?"

"We saved your darn life," Molly reminded the newly revived PlazHartz executive. "And I think this place I've rented is rather sedate and—"

"You and Dr. Windom had a disagreement earlier tonight," Jolson said, pointing at Larchmont from the sofa he was sharing with Molly.

"Well, yes."

"You've probably been getting somewhat unsettled by all the murders," he went on. "Too many of them, too frequently."

"S-s-she promised only t-t-two or th-th-three." Larchmont slumped in his slingchair. "B-b-but then Heather decided there was more d-d-deadwood than she'd originally realized."

"You suggested she stop altogether."

Larchmont nodded, tugging at his whiskers. "She seemed to agree, yet from what you're hinting—"

"This is way beyond a hint," said Molly. "She pixed the ServoBot factory, thought she was talking to you and said you were finished. Then she sent some sort of signal that activated one of those deadly Simon Lenz andies and sent him to wipe you out with a kilgun. If Ben hadn't been impersonating you and I hadn't walked through the wall when—"

"It does sound p-p-plausible, and yet I f-f-find it difficult to—"

"Put it to a test." Jolson stood, started pacing. "Go back to work tomorrow, walk right into your office. See what follows."

Larchmont tangled his fingers together. "I don't care, in the light of what you say's occurred, to r-r-risk that."

Molly said, "Then stay here in one of the guest rooms until this blows over and—"

"B-b-blows over? How's it going to—"

"We're going to stop the whole damn business," explained Jolson. "The killings, the mind controlling and all the—"

"B-b-but if Heather's brought to book, I'll be arrested, too," said Larchmont. "As an accessory, an accomplice to—"

"We'll see you get off," lied Molly.

"C-c-can you do that?"

"Sure," lied Jolson. "That is, if you cooperate."

"How?"

"First off, we want to know where Jennifer Lenz is."

"That p-p-poor young lass," sighed Larchmont.

"You do know where she's being held, don't you?" asked Molly. "You were, until tonight, Dr. Windom's right hand—"

"J-j-jennifer's over in Podengo Territory."

Jolson urged, "Be more specific."

"Heather owns a g-g-goodly portion of the Counter-Guerilla College in Podengo," said Larchmont. "That's the facility where dictators and juntas from all the Hell-quad planets send select troops and key m-m-military personnel to learn how to combat and destroy guerillas, insurgents, revolutionaries and other dangerous l-l-liberals."

"What part of the setup's she being held in?"

Looking down at his tangled fingers, Larchmont replied, "Heather stuck her in the War Nerves Clinic. That's where they treat soldiers and advisors who've c-c-cracked up in battle. I was very close to Simon Lenz at one time, and it p-p-pains me to think of his daughter—"

"Close until you and Dr. Windom and the rest decided he was a liability."

"Simon wouldn't go for the mind-control dodge that Heather came up with. The profits from controlling so many key people on Farpa, though, have been m-m-most impressive," Larchmont said with a small sad smile. "Alas, however, my conscience has s-s-started to—"

"That sometimes happens after the fourth or fifth killing," said Jolson.

CHAPTER 21

The slim young woman with the rainbow hair halted her stumbling progress down the aisle of the swaying railroad passenger car and squinted at Jolson. "Hey, I know you," she announced.

"No, you don't, sis."

Clutching her glopurse to her chest, she climbed over his fat legs and sat in the window seat. They were rolling through hot midday jungle. "Glory, what dippy scenics," she said. "Anyway, as I was saying, I recognize you. Sure, you're Bud Spooner."

Jolson said, "That puts you one up on me."

"Shoot, I keep forgetting to pass around my bizcard." From her cluttered purse she withdrew a talking card. "Here."

He took it, gingerly, between thumb and forefinger. "Actually, I could go this whole excursion without knowing who you—"

"INTRODUCING," boomed the voxcard, "MISS TIMMY TEMPEST, REPORTER AT LARGE FOR *GALACTIC VARIETY!*"

Holding the open purse under his hand, Timmy suggested, "Drop it in quick or it might fry your fingers. It tends to do that, but I guess you know from the way you're—"

"A lot of pushy kids have fobbed their cheap cards off on me over—"

"I'm no kid. I'm twenty."

"INTRODUCING TIMMY—"

She snapped the purse shut, muffling the voice of the enthusiastic business card. "Now then, as one pro to another, Spooner, suppose you tell me why one of the top comedians of yesteryear is taking this dippy journey through—"

"Who said you were a pro?" He scratched at his curly grey hair with pudgy fingers. "Who said I was from yesteryear? Do you have any idea what my universewide salary was last year alone?"

"Sure, you pulled down two hundred seventy thousand trubux," answered Timmy, smirking. "A drop of over three hundred thousand from the previous year, and that one was far from your best. It's really sort of pathetic how you washed-up guys cling to the notion—"

"I made three hundred seventy thousand last year. Which, sis, is about ten times what an underfed little bimbo like you—"

"Hey, I'm not a fading clown. I'm still on my way up," Timmy pointed out. "You know, you remind me of a rumdum agent I chanced to encounter on a recent—"

"Skip that," he said, "and fill me in on why a hotshot journalist like you is riding this Hellquad Quaint and Slow Transit System train across Podengo Territory."

"It's a fate worse than death," the rainbow-haired girl said, slouching and sneering out at the multiple shades of green they were rattling by. "See, I got assigned to do a two-hundred-sixty-word feature story on the *Counter-Guerilla Follies*. That's a dippy amateur show they're putting on at this cesspool called—"

"The Counter-Guerilla College," said Jolson in his nasal Bud Spooner voice. "I'm going there to emcee that particular festivity. Give it a little class. I'm also logged to lecture at the Troop Morale and Civilian Pacification Center on how to tell jokes under fire, warm up the troops, jolly the bombed-out civilians and—"

"Your name isn't on the poopsheet they faxed me."

"I'm a last-minute addition."

"You must really be on the skids," observed Timmy. "I'd heard you were supposed to be going on before the headline act at Cosmo's orbiting casino over in the—"

"That engagement's postponed." Actually the real Bud Spooner was out there, but nobody on the staff of the college was aware of the fact and Jolson'd been able to pass himself off as the venerable comedian and get invited to participate in tonight's show.

"I bet the gig fell through and they gave you the heave-ho."

"You don't seem to realize, sis, that throughout the universe the name Bud Spooner stands not only for top-flight comedy but for patriotic duty as well," he said. "Ever since the Murdstone space colony wars of twenty years ago I've been entertaining troops all across this—"

"Twenty years ago? Glory, you must be even older than you look, and that's going some."

Jolson looked beyond her, watching the jungle. Three green monkeys were cavorting high in the yellow-leaved trees. "Suppose you do a hundred-fifty-word yarn on me," he suggested. "I'm sure if you went to the public-relations officer at the college and told him what a great admirer of mine you—"

"I'd rather write about the Fleas." She gave a snorting laugh, dropped her purse to the floor and folded her arms under her breasts. "All I need for you is about a sentence. 'Old-time comic makes pathetic attempt to woo young audience.' Something like that. Anything more would be—"

From quite close up ahead came an enormous explosion.

The train rattled, shimmied and shrieked to a slow, jerky stop.

The train conductor was a long, lanky catman. "Just a temporary delay, folks," he said as he tromped through the thick, spiky brush that lined the tracks. "I suggest you all get back on board to await repairs on—"

"Temporary?" said Timmy, pointing beyond the halted engine of the HQSTS train. "The dippy bridge was just blown up."

"A crew is probably already on the way to repair the bridge, miss. Why, by nightfall we'll be zooming along like—"

"And what about these?" Letting go of Jolson's arm, she waved a leaflet at the conductor.

There were dozens of the bright yellow sheets of faxpaper scattered along the tracks, lying on the loamy earth, dangling from bushes. Several of the milling passengers were picking them up and perusing them. A plump birdboy was making an airplane out of one.

The conductor said, "Nothing but propaganda."

"It says, and I quote, 'DEATH to all supporters of the

fascist Counter-Guerilla College! DEATH to all who ride trains that travel in that direction!' "

The conductor removed his gilded cap, rubbed at his furry head. "Yes, propaganda is usually phrased that way."

"So if we sit on that train, we'll probably get blown up like—"

"Attention, all passengers," said voxboxes strung to the cars. "Tractorbuses will be arriving shortly to carry you comfortably on the remaining ten miles of your journey. Please step back inside the train cars to await their arrival. Our refreshment car is now serving three kinds of sandwiches—including grout loaf on Venusian soldier's bread, my own personal favorite—and a tempting variety of beverages."

"I wish they'd told me about the buses," said the conductor.

"C'mon, sis," said Jolson. "Let's go park our tokes."

"We'll be just like sitting snergs," Timmy said. "Targets for a bunch of wild-eyed propagandists."

"Talk about your fates worse than death," grumbled Timmy, fanning herself with her lumpy glopurse. "Bumping along the back roads of the boonies in a sweltering landbus, accompanied by an overage funnyman and a bunch of sappy goons who claim to be something called the Hellquad String Quartet."

"You could, if you were a true reporter, get a heck of a story out of this unexpected adventure, sis," Jolson told her.

"Hooey. I wouldn't even write up something this dull and dippy in my annual letter to my ancient granny on the planet Barafunda."

The four dogmen who made up the string group were sitting in front and in back of Jolson and the young reporter on the small two-dozen-seat passenger bus.

The violinist, who had the window seat in front, turned his muzzle toward Timmy. "Our lives are filled with exciting incidents like this."

"Nertz," she replied, giving her attention to the muddy road the tractorbus was rumbling over. Thick-trunked trees rose high on both sides.

"We can tell you, for example, about the time we rescued the baby from being carried off by an eagle." The cellist, occupying the window seat to the rear, tapped Jolson's pudgy shoulder with a well-manicured paw.

"You lads have the wrong man," he told them. "I'm not with the press, only the young lady. I am merely an old doddering minstrel, a faded—"

"You still look quite spry," said the cellist.

"He's being sarcastic," explained Timmy, digging a pack of ExploGum from her purse.

Jolson hunched slightly, trying to see up and out. "Hush for a moment, sis."

"Me hush? Why, glory, every washed-up showbum on this rattletrap has been babbling to me since we began this jittery journey—POP! POP! POW!—trying to get me to write up their shabby careers in the influential pages of— POPPITY POP! POW!—my newspaper."

"Swallow that damn gum." He leaned further across her, gazing out. He was looking up into the glaring afternoon sky.

"What the dickens are you doing, sprawling all over me? If you think physical contact with your dumpy old carcass—POPPO! WOPPO! WOPPO!—is going to arouse any—"

"Silence. Take a gander up there."

She looked. "Glory, we're being followed by skyrods."

There were three souped-up skycars flying low overhead. Painted dazzling basic colors, scribbled over with slogans—DEATH TO IMPERIALISTS! WARPIGS MUST DIE! TYRANS HAVE TO GO!

"What kind of rebels are they? Don't even know how to spell *tyrants.*"

"Driver," called Jolson to the fat catman at the controls. "You better make for cover."

Cupping a paw to a shaggy ear, the driver requested, "Say that again."

"Looks like we may be attacked." He jerked a thumb skyward.

"Jumping jellybeans!" The bus came to an abrupt, clattering stop. The furry driver yanked the door release, grabbed up his lunchbox and fled out into the surrounding jungle.

Reaching across the young woman, Jolson pushed the escape button on the emergency door. "I picked this particular seat just in case." The door popped free, tumbling out into the tangle of brush and hairy vines roadside. "Out this way." He shoved her.

Timmy flew from the stopped bus. "I didn't need that powerful a nudge," she said, landing in the midst of a twisting flowering bush.

"Folks, you all better get off the bus," said Jolson, illustrating his point by diving clear.

The trio of skyrods was circling now, dropping even lower.

He extricated Timmy from the landscape, got her upright and led her swiftly away from the sitting tractorbus.

They went dodging around tree trunks, hopping over great gnarled vines.

Roughly three minutes later the bombs began hitting the bus.

CHAPTER 22

The public-relations lieutenant was a tall, straight catwoman in a two-piece grey unisuit. "You two are the first survivors of the alleged rebel raid to come straggling in. We expect—"

"What do you mean, *alleged?*" Timmy wiped at her perspiring forehead with the heel of her hand. "Those dinks blew up our bus and—"

"I was," said the public-relations lieutenant, "using *alleged* to modify *rebel,* not *raid.* It's our belief that most of these so-called rebels are financed by off-planet forces who—"

"Sis, can we get in out of the weather?" asked Jolson.

They were standing outside the grey, domed public-relations building. It was late afternoon, the sky a glaring yellow over the twenty-acre walled Counter-Guerilla College campus.

"Of course, Mr. Spooner. Forgive me for waxing ideological." She made a small stiff bow in his direction. "I'll escort you and the young lady to the Guest Barracks. It's but a short walk."

"Better be." Timmy walked close beside Jolson as they followed the uniformed public-relations officer along a grey gravel path. "You're in better shape than you look, Spooner."

"Sure," he agreed.

"We climbed over hills and through ravines getting here across that dippy jungle," the rainbow-haired girl said, panting some. "And you're fresh as a meech flower, while I'm near gedunked."

"No doubt, sis, it's the riotous life you lead."

"Bunk. I happen to lead a spotless life and follow the diet plans laid out in *Galactic Vegetarian Times*. Nope, I think there's something not quite on the—"

"Perhaps you'd best cover your ears for a moment," suggested the public-relations lieutenant. They were passing a high grey brix wall.

"Why's that, sis?"

The catwoman explained, "We've found most visitors don't like to hear executions."

"Is somebody getting conked off on the other side of this wall?" Timmy's eyes went wide.

"Four gentlemen actually, in approximately one minute," answered the catwoman. "Oh, and I should've mentioned this before, Mr. Spooner, it has something to do with you."

"Does it, now?"

The public-relations lieutenant continued striding briskly along. "Yes, since it's going to mean you'll have to rearrange the lineup of the show this evening."

Zzzzzzitttttzzzzzz!

Timmy yelped at the sound of the kilgun from the other side of the wall. She grabbed hold of Jolson's arm, squeezed.

Zzzzzittzzzzzz!

"We'd scheduled a highly touted group called the Comedy Commandos for the *Follies,*" said the catwoman. "These four gentlemen arrived and claimed to be the Comedy Commandos."

Zzzzzitttzzzzzz!

Jolson inquired, "But they weren't?"

"They turned out, after a very simple check of their ID packets, to be impostors. Rebels, no doubt."

Zzzzzitttzzzzz!

He cleared his throat and said nothing.

After they'd passed the wall and two more grey, domed buildings, the catwoman lieutenant stopped in front of a grey, domed building. "This is the Guest Barracks," she said. "You'll each have a comfortable private suite."

"Very ritzy," murmured Timmy, shivering.

"Oh, and let me apologize in advance," the public-relations lieutenant said. "The barracks happen to be right next to the War Nerves Clinic over there. Some of our visitors are uneasy by the proximity to—"

"It won't," Jolson assured her, "bother me in the least."

Jolson went for a quiet stroll soon after the day faded away. High floating globes of light made the grey gravel paths fairly bright. He paused in the shadows of a stand of stunted trees, watching the brightly lit front of the clinic. A broad-shouldered grey guardbot stood on the ramp that led to the main entrance.

"I thought so."

Turning slowly, he saw Timmy standing behind him. "Vacate," he advised.

"Hooey," she replied. "You're up to something sneaky, Spooner. In fact, you are maybe not even Spooner."

"I'm Spooner. Go away."

"Not that I'd want to see them stick you against the

wall," she said, shivering. "But, being a crackerjack investigative reporter, I have tumbled to you."

"Toddle over to the auditorium, sis. Otherwise you may not get a seat."

"I sense a big story in the making here. Something definitely front-page, running four hundred words or better."

"I'm taking a walk before I go over to emcee the show." He dropped his right hand into the pocket of his jacket. "That is, absolutely, all that's occurring hereabouts."

"Suppose I tag along."

"I'm polishing my opening monologue. That requires lots of solitude."

"Nertz. I intend to dog your footsteps."

"Okay, then I may as well level with you." He gave a sigh of resignation. "Here, I'll show you something."

Zzzzzzzummmmmmm!

What had come swiftly out of his pocket was his stungun. Before Timmy realized that, the beam had hit her just below the left breast.

She rose up on tiptoe, made a hazy swatting motion with her right hand. She went rigid, then fell forward against him.

He lifted her up in both arms, ran for the War Nerves Clinic. He trotted up the ramp, remembering to pant the way a man in Spooner's general shape would.

"Stop right there, sir." The guardbot pointed his stungun finger at Jolson.

"This is an emergency," he gasped as he came tottering right up to the entrance with the unconscious girl. "My assistant in the *Follies* has just been stricken with the worst case of stage fright I've ever seen."

"You're implying this is some sort of medical emergency?"

"It surely is."

"Very well." The guardbot moved away from the grey plaz door. "Go on in and take corridor B."

The door hissed open. Jolson huffed inside with his burden and deposited her on the first medicot he sighted.

Returning to his own person, Jolson opened the door of the small grey room and went in. "This is a rescue, Miss Lenz."

The thin, red-haired young woman was sitting on the floating grey cot, arms dangling at her sides. She looked up at him with hazy eyes. "I thought I heard something just fall over in the corridor."

"Your guardbot."

Nodding, Jennifer asked, "And who are you?"

He crossed the grey floor to her. "An operative with the Briggs Interplanetary Detective Service."

"Lately," she admitted, stroking her cheek with her fingertips, "I'm never quite sure what to believe or whom to trust."

"I suggest you put your faith in me," he told her. "Otherwise we may both get stuck in this hoosegow. I've had to stun or disable seven or eight staff members, humanoid and mechanical, to get up here to you. Plus a lady journalist and a guy who was delivering towels. That won't go unnoticed forever."

Jennifer said, "Have you told me your name?"

"It's Ben Jolson. Now we have to—"

"Your clothes don't fit so well."

"There's an interesting explanation for that, which I'll tell you outside of here."

Slowly and carefully, she stood up. "Forgive me for not making much sense, Mr. Jolson," she said, brushing her red hair back from her pale face. "They've been trying out some new pacifying drugs on me all this week. The newest one should wear off in a few more hours and I'll be back to normal. Or what I think is normal these days."

Putting an arm around her shoulders, he walked her to the doorway. "There are some skyambulances docked out back."

"Yes, I know. They brought me here in one, strapped down."

"We'll borrow one."

She glanced down at the big gunmetal guardbot sprawled in the hall. "Where are we going?"

"Our initial goal is to get the hell out of here." He hurried her along to a grey downramp.

"That'll be nice," she said.

CHAPTER 23

Jolson sat slightly hunched in the driveseat of the rented landcar. Thunder rumbled far off; rain began falling down across the grey dawn and pelting the pale green hood. Lightning sizzled through the quirky back streets of Danger Zone #15, illuminating the arched doorways and the huddled figures. At the mouth of a zigzag alley a lean yellow dog was sniffing at a sprawled birdman. Further along three raggedy catkids were playing a toss game with an empty wine plazflask.

After making a frightened murmuring sound, Jennifer awakened and straightened in the seat. "We're back in the capital," she recognized after glancing around for a moment.

"The lesser outskirts. How're you doing?"

The thin young woman brushed at her hair with her left hand. "I'm feeling," she answered, "almost like myself. How far are we from your friend's villa?"

"My employer's villa," he corrected.

"From the way you spoke about Molly Briggs, I'd guess she's a close friend as well."

"We're about fifteen miles from the place."

Jennifer said, "Right now, you know, I'm not sure of

151

the state of my finances. Eventually, however, I'll see to it that your agency is paid all—"

"I can't say we aren't in it for the money. But we're also interested in straightening out this whole mess," he said. "You have to do that when people try to kill you."

"It's an enormous mess, too," she said. "I'm afraid I fell asleep before you got to explain everything, Ben. Because of the drugs they used on me, that usually happens."

"Dr. Windom seems to be in charge of most of the trouble," he said, swerving to avoid two fat dogmen who were squabbling in the street over the ownership of an ancient pair of snergskin boots. "With Lou Killdozer contributing some blackmail and flimflamming on the side."

"Heather Windom, yes," she said quietly. "I never did care much for her—and I guess it was mutual, considering all she's done to me these past few years."

"You knew what she was up to, the business with the mind-control drug in selected plaz hearts?"

"Father found out about that, and he told me. Heather was certain he'd never go along with anything like that . . . and . . . and she got some of the others to agree with her that my father had to be . . . to be . . . taken care of."

"Nowadays she isn't too happy with her original group of conspirators."

"I got that much from you last night," said Jennifer. "So she rigged those androids of mine to kill the ones she no longer trusts."

"Eventually she was going to frame you for the whole job, soon as she'd wiped out enough of her cronies."

Jennifer leaned back. "I imagine I was supposed to commit suicide, leaving a note taking blame for all the deaths and saying I'd used my own androids to revenge my father."

"Sure, that's why she removed you from the Mad-house Spa. That'd be written off as an escape when the time came," he said. "You'd be found here in the city."

"I wonder if I could really have done something like that," she said thoughtfully. "Sent those andies out to kill the people responsible for my father's death."

"Even if you call it revenge, it's still murder. And most folks can't do that."

"I was very fond of my father, though," she said.

Eyes narrowing, Jolson said, "Stay here."

"You think something's wrong?" asked Jennifer, nodding at the brightly lit villa.

"Might be." He eased out of the parked landcar into the early-morning rain.

He drew out his stungun as he approached the house. The front door, which he'd noticed as soon as they'd driven onto the grounds, was open wide. Jammed, apparently. Lights seemed to be on in every room, glaring out into the grey of the new day.

Jolson halted a few feet from the bright doorway. The rain hit at him as he stood, watchful, and listened.

After a minute he rushed forward, diving across the threshold. He stopped, standing wide-legged and scanning the big living room.

A slingchair lay with its legs in the air. One of the floating globe lamps had fallen and smashed in front of the fireplace.

Jolson called, "Molly?"

The rain pattered at the high, wide windows.

"Molly?"

He realized he didn't expect an answer and didn't bother to call her name again.

She wasn't in the master bedroom. Another chair was overturned, and sprawled on the floor beside it were Molly's antigrav belt and her wallwalking gear.

"She never goes out without that stuff," he murmured.

There was no trace of Larchmont in any of the guest rooms, though in one room the floating bed had dropped down onto its base.

Alongside the askew bed were several small rust-brown spots.

"Looks like somebody grabbed him. But how'd they know he was here?"

Maybe Larchmont had told them. The PlazHartz executive wasn't the most trustworthy guy around, and it could be he'd contacted Dr. Windom to make an attempt to ingratiate himself back into the mind-control business.

In the kitchen Jolson found something else. Spread out flat on his back on the yellow floor was Buster. The robot's glaz eyes were wide open, glowing dimly red. The left side of his metal head had been smashed in.

Jennifer took a step back from the dining-room table. "I haven't done this kind of work in quite a while," she said, rubbing at the corner of her eye with her wrist. "But he seems to be about patched up."

"Just so Buster can talk to me." Jolson nodded at the robot on the table. "And tell me what happened to Molly."

Jennifer picked up an electro-screwdriver and finished putting Buster's repaired skull back together. "It was fortunate that Miss Briggs had this case of electrotools in her luggage."

"If it's a gadget, she's likely to have it. That's why I suggested we check out her luggage."

"She paid too much for it, though."

"How do you know what she paid?"

"Price tag is still on the case." Jennifer backed off again. "There. He ought to be okay now."

Jolson leaned over the robot. "Buster."

The robot's metal elbows thumped the polished neo-wood table as he thrashed from side to side a few times. "Huh? Who's paging me?" He opened his eyes, frowned up at Jolson. "Is that youse, Jolson?"

"It is," he said. "Chameleon."

"Yeah, and youse got the password."

"Tell me what happened here."

Creaking some, the robot sat up. "Who's the bean-pole?"

"You concentrate on telling me—"

"And somebody's been dorking around with my bean."

"I patched you up," Jennifer told him. "You're still going to need a complete overhaul before—"

"Hey, that's right. They bopped me on the coco," remembered Buster.

Jolson asked, "Who?"

"Couple of runty birdmen. Can youse imagine that? Yeah, they used a disabler first. Then one of them goes to work on my noggin with a crowbar."

"Who were they?"

"I ain't absolute sure, but I figure they must be working for Dr. Windom."

"Okay, start filling me in," said Jolson, impatience showing in his voice. "Where's Molly?"

Buster tapped the side of his ball head with his finger-tips. "I guess I gotta take the rap for some of this," he said. "See, I was tailing Sally like youse told me."

"And?"

"I figure Sally and that bozo with the pansy whiskers got wise," explained the chagrined robot. "This Molly skirt pixes me in my jalopy, slips me the password and says to come here to report to her. Also she's thinking maybe I can guard some dunk name of Larchmont."

"What you're leading up to," said Jolson, "is that Sally followed you here?"

"Her and the blond gink who looks sort of like Lou, yeah." Buster nodded his head, producing a faint squeaking. "Sally pushes right in, starts hollering at Molly. 'Geez, ain't this business built on mutual trust?' and similar sentiments."

"How's Dr. Windom figure in this?"

"This here is conjecture on my part," said the robot. "But about five minutes after Sally and the blond chump barges in here, about a half dozen or more thugs bust in. They're packing stunguns, disablers, kilguns and a whole stewpot of other such hardware. I happen to be pottering in the kitchen, mixing up some herb tea for Molly and—wham! Them two birdmen use a disabler on me and then try to bash my brains in."

"Windom's minions," said Jolson, "and they must've gotten wise to Sally and her sidekick's watching them. They trailed them here."

"I feel like a jerk," confessed Buster.

Jolson said, "Well, it seems it's time we paid a visit to Dr. Windom."

CHAPTER 24

They came strolling across the garden courtyard of the hotel. Jolson was in the lead, flipping a one-trubuck coin with his copper right hand. Jennifer followed close behind him, wearing a blond wig and a short-skirted crimson cazdress. Buster, who was now painted a glittery silver, came rumbling along last, carrying several large suitcases.

"Youse went too far with this disguise stuff, Jolson," he was grumbling.

"Be still," advised the young woman, "or you'll give us away."

"Only a pansy'd go around coated with silver."

"Silence," said Jolson as they entered the two-story-high lobby.

He swaggered over to the boomerang-shaped desk that floated between two potted yellow palm trees.

"Welcome, sir." A blonde android sat behind the registration desk. She appeared to weigh close to three hundred pounds and wore a gem-studded one-piece glittergown. "Lest you become confused, allow me to explain that I am not actually Lulu Sunnyside but rather a cleverly constructed android replica of that famous lady."

"Second-rate workmanship," Jennifer whispered to Jolson.

"How's that, my dear?"

Jolson rubbed his aluminum nose with a flesh finger. "She says she hopes you get over the spiel pretty soon so as we can get to our suite, honey."

The fat android gave him a dimpled smile. "Most of our guests at the Sunnyside Garden Hotel—one of ninety-three splendorous Sunnyside Hotels to serve you in this planet system and one of four hundred sixty-seven Sunnyside Hotels in the whole wide universe—most of our contented guests, I say, are delighted to know that in each and every Sunnyside Hotel they'll be greeted by a lovely replica of Lulu Sunnyside herself and—"

"You come into all these hotels by marrying the old coot who owned them, didn't you?" Resting his seemingly metal hand on the desk, he leaned toward her. "Hurford E. Sunnyside, who died soon after the ceremony. Might've been he conked out while trying to heft your carcass over the threshold of—"

"Sir, I am commencing to wonder if you and your party are really the sort of guests we want at—"

"Yeah, we're your kind of guests," Jolson assured her. "Nobody ever cancels my reservation. I'm Johnny Mechanix."

The android blinked. "Oops," she remarked. "Would you be the selfsame Johnny Mechanix who controls organized crime in the Trinidad System of planets and came by his colorful nickname because as various parts of him got shot, blasted and zapped away he replaced them and became ever more of a cyborg, dedicated to destroying his enemies?"

"That's me, yeah. Now what say you hustle us up a

suite," he said. "For me and my lady friend and my valet."

"Yes, Mr. Mechanix. If you'll just sign the little faxcard that's coming up through the slot there."

"My valet takes care of stuff like that. Bertie, sign us in."

"Bertie? How come you stick a . . . that is, very well, sir. At once, sir."

Jolson stepped back from the desk. "You ought to be safe here," he told Jennifer. "Now that everybody knows about the villa, we can't use it anymore."

"I ought to come with you while you're trying to find out where Dr. Windom's taken Molly Briggs and the others."

"Nope, it's better if I work alone on that."

"Eventually," she said, "I'm going to help."

Jolson, himself at the moment, picked up the snoring catman by the collar and the seat of his tattered trousers and lifted him off the park bench. Jolson carried him a dozen yards, deposited him on the weedy grass near the trunk of a dying tree.

Dusting his hands, he returned to the bench and sat. The snores of the catman drifted over to him.

Three ragged musicians came shuffling along the path. They halted in front of the bench, and the dogman with the cornet inquired, "In the mood for a serenade?"

"On the contrary." He extracted a trubux coin from his jacket pocket. "But I'll finance your traveling elsewhere."

"Am I to take it you're not a fan of Martian-style Dixieland?"

"You're to take it that I'm giving you a dollar to pre-serve my solitude."

"A deal." The leader held out a paw.

The lizardman trombonist dropped his already dented instrument twice before they wandered out of sight.

"Since we're meeting in the park, I thought a nice picnic basket would be in order." Dr. IQ hurried up, sat beside Jolson and rested a large yellow neowicker hamper on his knees. "I've got sandwiches made with cream cheese, Port Salut, Camembert, Munster—"

"Skip the menu," Jolson advised the ratman. "I'm anxious to hear whatever information you've come up with."

IQ sighed, adjusted his knit cap and leaned to set the hamper on the ground. "You miss a lot of life's joys, Ben, by being so dedicated to your work," he said, reaching inside his overcoat with a mittened hand. "What you have to do is relax and savor life's pleasures while there's time." He brought out a folded sheet of green faxpaper.

"Have you found out where Heather Windom is holding them?"

"That wasn't all that difficult, given my knack and contacts," the ratman said as he unfurled the sheet. "Dr. Windom brought your Miss Briggs and the others to the Lenz mansion late last evening."

"That's where Jennifer and her father used to live?"

"The same abode, yes, Ben. Dr. Windom's been using it off and on since she railroaded Jennifer into the hatch."

"Any word on what she's planning to do with them?"

Bending, Dr. IQ reached into the hamper. "Eventually that lady tends to kill everybody." He selected a plyowrapped sandwich. "I'm only guessing, but I fear it doesn't look so good for Miss Briggs."

"Where's the mansion located?"

"In a very fancy Safe Zone at the edge of the capital, overlooking a very scenic lake. The property values thereabouts have been skyrocketing these past few—"

"I'll have to get in there."

Dr. IQ had unwrapped the sandwich with mittened fingers. "Ar, this is that Brie I was telling you about," he said, chuckling. "You sure you won't pause to enjoy a—"

"Maybe afterwards." Jolson stood. "Thanks, Doc."

"It all goes on the tab," said the ratman. "But, Ben, you really ought to think about taking it—"

"If I need anything else, I'll pix you." He went hurrying away.

Jennifer spread the map out on the Lucite coffee table. "All right, here's our home, right here on this part of the lakeshore." Pausing, she sniffed. "What's that odd odor, Ben?"

"Cheese. I'll explain at a future date."

"Smelling like ripe cheese ain't half so bad as being daubed silver," muttered the robot, who was sitting on a rubberoid sofa and scowling down at the outspread map.

"I'll see you get a complete overhaul and are buffed back to your original state," promised the red-haired Jennifer. "Soon as we take care of Dr. Windom."

Leaning over the kneeling young woman, Jolson pointed at the map. "You say there's another way to get inside the place?"

"Yes, and one I'm sure Heather knows nothing about," she said. "It sounds rather . . . well, like something a very indulgent father would do for a spoiled daughter. At any rate, Father had a special tunnel built. There's a secret entrance in the wardrobe closet of my bedroom. Then the tunnel runs under about a half mile of the shore and comes out in the basement storeroom of Miss Robinson's School for Girls." She touched the map. "And that's right there."

"Miss Robinson went along with all this?"

Jennifer looked up and smiled. "My father was a very important man, and a generous supporter of the school," she said. "And this was, Ben, not as impractical as you might think. The tunnel meant I could get safely to school and back every day without being bothered by potential kidnappers or reporters or any of the other annoyances a rich man's daughter might be subjected to. But, of course, the main reason he did it was because I felt—back when I was eleven—that the idea of a secret tunnel was just wonderful."

"All we have to do, then," said Jolson, "is get into the school and use the tunnel to get into the mansion."

"Yes, and I'm certain Miss Robinson won't have any object—"

"Youse better hold it." Buster had his ball head out over the map. He tapped a spot with his metal forefinger. "Is this where that school is supposed to be?"

"Yes, right there." Jennifer frowned.

"Hell, they moved out a year ago," the mechanical man said. "A whole new establishment is there now."

"Who?" asked Jolson.

"It's called Computer Mama's," replied the robot. "It's a very ritzy bordello."

CHAPTER 25

Buster was piloting their rented skycar through the clear night. "When I was aiding and abetting Lou Killdozer," he complained, "I never had to go around looking like no nancy."

"Nobody can see you at this altitude," pointed out Jolson, who was once again the cyborg Johnny Mechanix.

"*I* can see me."

"Behave yourself, Buster." Jennifer straightened her blond wig as she gazed down through the seethru glaz floor. "The old neighborhood has changed."

There were a great many lights gleaming on the lakeshore below, bright signs announcing restaurants, cabarets, bistros and casinos. Docked on the dark waters were three neon-trimmed gambling barges.

"Bingo." Buster put the skycar into a gradual descent pattern. "There's Computer Mama's."

"I don't see it," said Jennifer.

"The only joint with no lights at all," said the robot. "It's so classy they don't have no sign."

"Once you set us down," reminded Jolson, "scoot on over to the rendezvous spot and wait."

"I'll wait," said Buster, "but I ain't got all that much faith in youse."

The apeman in the three-piece tuxsuit adjusted his monocle once again. "I fear you've misunderstood the nature of our enterprise, sir," he said, looking Jolson and Jennifer up and down in turn. "We sell, we don't purchase. Further, Computer Mama's is staffed entirely by a wide variety of lovely *android* ladies and thus—"

"Listen." Jolson poked him on the chest with two copper fingers. "I don't like being patronized by my inferiors. You get me? Secondly, this broad *is* an android. A sample of the kind of goods I'm prepared to provide this joint."

"I'm truly sorry if I've offended you, sir," said the apeman, taking two steps back across the ebony floor of the foyer. "However, we never deal with unsolicited vendors of—"

"If you keep playing around with that eyeglass, fella, it's going to get inserted in another portion of your anatomy," warned Jolson. "Now you go trotting off to your boss and you tell him that Johnny Mechanix is cooling his heels out in this goddamn lobby with a working model of the greatest breakthrough in robotics since—"

"Oops." The monocle popped free. "Not the same Johnny Mechanix who controls all organized crime in the Trinidads and came by his quaint nickname because as various portions of him got shot, blasted and zapped away he replaced them and became more and more a cyborg?"

"Yeah, that's me," admitted Jolson. "I got a real short temper, too, and I passed the limit of it about a minute and a half ago, so unless—"

"I'm certain Mr. Metz will be more than pleased to meet with you, Mr. Mechanix." The apeman smiled carefully. "Will you and the young lady . . . that is, you and your demonstration model follow me."

Taking hold of Jennifer's bare left arm, he escorted her along after the apeman.

They walked a wide pink-lit corridor to a cream-colored door.

The apeman knocked twice, then three times more.

"Yeah?" came a foggy voice out of the voxbox in mid-door.

"Someone to see you, Mr. Metz."

"I don't want to see no one."

"This happens to be Johnny Mechanix."

"Oops."

"Mr. Metz?"

"Show the guy in."

The door slid aside. Jolson and Jennifer entered and the apeman withdrew. The door slid shut.

Seated behind a wide ivory desk was a man in a tuxsuit, top hat and black neosilk face mask.

"Hi, Freddie," said Jolson, dragging Jennifer across the room with him.

"Nix on calling me Freddie," said Metz. "What I mean is, on this planet they all know me as Mysterious Metz. It's a sort of, you know, advertising gimmick. Mysterious Metz. Gives the yokels an extra thrill when they patronize Computer Mama's. Freddie Metz, on the other hand, don't have any zing in that direction."

"Sure thing, Mysterious." Jolson let go of the young woman and then pointed proudly at her. "Looks real, don't she?"

"Of course, because she is real."

"Naw, she's an andy."

"Groutcrap. You can't get skin color like that with—"

"Did I spacejump here all the way from the damn Trinidads to play a prank on you?"

Metz tugged at the hem of his mask. "Android, huh?"

"The most believable one yet put on the market. I got the exclusive marketing of—"

"I hope you won't take no offense, Johnny," interrupted Metz, "but how come you built her so skinny?"

"Not skinny, Mysterious. Svelte." He motioned the young woman to turn around once.

"Well, call her svelte or skinny. She ain't got much in the yonkers department and is in the possession of a toke that leaves much to be desired."

"Where you been? Don't you know the trend today is toward slim women? Sure, a recent report in *Hooker Wholesaler* states that—"

"This ain't the Barnum System, Johnny. On Farpa they still like them on the chunky side."

"Okay, so we can build you some fat ones," Jolson conceded. "The point is—"

The pixphone on one side of Mysterious Metz's desk started bleating in an anguished way.

"Excuse me, Johnny. Yeah? Mysterious Metz speaking."

"Mr. Metz, sir," came the voice of the apeman, "I took the liberty of checking up on your visitor. Rather interestingly, I've learned that the true and authentic Johnny Mechanix is, as we speak, still residing on one of the Trinidad planets."

"Tell him to come on in here," suggested Jolson, showing his kilgun to the masked man.

The tunnel was chill and smelled of damp earth. The pale yellow walls were streaked with greenish mildew.

"Seems obvious nobody's used this for quite some time," said Jennifer, who was walking close beside Jolson.

He held a lightrod in his hand. "Floor looks untrodden."

They moved slowly ahead into the darkness.

"Does that happen often?" she asked. "Where somebody sees through one of your impersonations?"

Jolson had returned to his natural self once again. "Now and then," he replied. "On such occasions I usually have to rely on such weapons as a stungun, as we just did up in Computer Mama's."

"I'm almost certain Mysterious Metz broke something when he fell over unconscious."

"That's but one of the hazards of being a mystery man."

They continued on in silence for several minutes.

"Funny," the young woman said, "I'm not feeling very sentimental. Yet I traveled through this tunnel almost every day for years."

"Probably you've outgrown it." He slowed. "We're nearing the other end."

"All right," she said. "After we go through the second door we'll be in the wardrobe closet of my old room."

"I know. You drew me a floor plan of the whole place."

"It's likely Dr. Windom's not using the upper floor. My guess is she's mostly utilizing the main floor and my father's lab."

"Meaning we ought to be able to sneak up on them."

Stopping in front of a blank section of pale yellow wall,

Jennifer crouched slightly to press her right hand to a spot just below midpoint. "I wasn't this tall then."

The panel slid silently open.

Beyond it stretched a short ramp.

They climbed up it, and the red-haired young woman pressed her palm to another panel.

That slid aside.

Her clothes were still hanging in long rows in the large wardrobe closet.

Jolson clicked off the lightrod and followed her to the closed door of the closet.

Taking a deep breath, Jennifer opened the door.

"This has saved me considerable effort, child." Dr. Windom, lean and blonde, was standing in the center of the room holding a kilgun.

CHAPTER 26

Dr. Windom pointed the kilgun briefly at Jolson. "You must be Ben Jolson."

"Didn't realize you'd heard of me." He came all the way into the blue-walled bedroom.

"Molly Briggs mentioned your name," she said, "eventually."

"I'd like to see her," he said evenly.

"That'll happen shortly," the blonde, white-clad woman promised. "Initially, though, I need Jenny to lend a—"

"Nobody calls me Jenny."

"I do, dear. I can call you anything I please."

Jennifer's red hair brushed her shoulders when she shook her head. "There's no reason why I should help you with anything," she said. "You're going to kill me anyway."

"Not yet, child." The doctor smiled thinly. "I'm nowhere near ready for that."

"Meaning you haven't finished bumping off your colleagues?" inquired Jolson.

"Unfortunately, no. The weeding process has turned out to be more extensive than I'd originally imagined."

"Won't be any of the thirteen left."

"Perhaps."

Jennifer said, "Once you're through using my androids, you'll arrange my death. Make it seem a suicide."

"Yes, that's right, dear," said Dr. Windom, the sparse smile again touching her face. "We have a wonderful vidtape confession and suicide message of you all ready to—"

"But I never—"

"You did, Jenny. Dr. Ripperger made it for us at the Madhouse Spa," the doctor explained to her. "Possibly you don't recall, since you were drugged at the time. Myself, I think your wild, glassy-eyed appearance adds to the mood of the thing."

Folding her arms, the young woman said, "You'll have to kill me now, because I have no intention of—"

"It's not you I'll kill, dear." She swung the kilgun toward Jolson once more. "I need you to assist me in repairing the android your friends damaged when they broke into my warehouse. If you don't agree, I'll shoot Jolson here and now."

Jennifer looked from the silvery tip of the kilgun to Jolson's face. "All right," she said quietly.

The one-way seethru glaz wall of the large laboratory showed the night grounds of the Lenz estate. Thin moonlight touched the overgrown lawns and unkempt hedges.

Jennifer said, "You haven't taken care of things."

"He's on the table," said Dr. Windom, gesturing with her kilgun.

In the center of the lab was a floating table, illuminated by dangling yellow light globes. Stretched out on the table was a red-haired Simon Lenz andy. Part of the torso had been reconstructed and the head reattached to the body.

Slowly Jennifer made a circuit of the table. "How'd you know we were in my room?" she asked.

"I became aware of that tunnel several months ago, dear. I thought it best to rig an alarm."

"This house has more than one secret." The girl stopped, reached out to touch the metal ribs of the injured android. "I can repair him, but it'll take time. Quite a lot of time."

"I'll allow you that, and you can begin right now." Dr. Windom settled into a glaz slingchair, resting her kilgun on her narrow lap. "Jolson, make a try at assisting her. I assume you're capable of at least low-level technical—"

"The lower the better." He rested his left buttock against the table, watching the seated doctor and the kilgun she was no longer gripping.

Jennifer crossed to the nearest wall. Several low pale green cabinets were lined up there. Kneeling, she blew the dust from the glaz doors. "Most of my tools and equipment are still here."

"Just as you left them, Jenny."

Jennifer stood, smiling. "There's one secret you didn't discover," she said. She pressed her hand casually against the wall just above one of the cabinets.

A rectangular panel slid swiftly aside.

From the compartment beyond Jennifer grabbed out a kilgun.

"You killed my father," she said and fired at Dr. Windom.

CHAPTER 27

Zzzzzittttzzzzzz!

Dr. Windom was still reaching for her own kilgun when the beam from Jennifer's touched her.

It ate away her throat, very quickly. Her blonde head fell free of her body, dropped into her lap and then tumbled to the floor along with the silvery kilgun her thin fingers were still clutching for.

Jolson moved now. He bent and, gingerly, grabbed up the doctor's fallen gun.

Then he went to Jennifer and put an arm around her. "Easy now," he said, "easy."

"I never," she said in the voice she must've had ten years before, "thought I'd ever kill anyone."

"How come that kilgun was in the hole in the wall?"

"What?"

"The kilgun. How'd you know it was there?"

Jennifer stared at the kilgun she was holding. "My father put it there. Years ago." Her voice was moving back closer to her real one. "In case anyone broke in on us here."

"The panel recognizes your handprint?"

She nodded, much too vigorously. "Mine and my father's."

"Good thing it was still in there."

"I gambled it would be," she said. "The minute Heather mentioned my helping her, I knew she meant to bring us to the lab."

"So you pretended to be against that."

"Yes, so she wouldn't suspect I was really very eager to get in here and at that concealed kilgun." She pulled free of him, looking into his eyes. "Aren't you going to comfort me? Tell me I did the right thing and not to feel bad about taking a life?"

"You already know that."

"But it wouldn't hurt to be—"

"Bullshit is not my specialty," he said. "At least not when I'm being myself. Dr. Windom was going to kill us, you killed her first. That's it, it's over and done. You're a grown-up Jennifer Lenz, not an andy dupe of Jenny at twelve. I don't have to pat you on the head and be paternal."

The young woman sighed. "You're right, Ben, you don't." She tucked the kilgun into her pocket. "Now we'd better find Molly Briggs before Heather's henchmen find us."

The toadman dropped right over, face first, onto the pebbled downramp.

Jolson tugged the guard's stungun from its holster, passed it to Jennifer. "Now you have a stungun of your own."

She took it in her left hand. "You're very good at sneaking up on people."

"One of my specialties."

"We've done pretty well thus far," she said as they

continued down toward the basement rooms of the mansion. "Two catmen, one guardbot, two toadmen and—"

"One catman," he corrected. "That other lad was a ratman."

"Was he? He fell over so rapidly I guess I didn't get a good look at him."

"Let's continue our descent in silence."

The first two storerooms they came to were unlocked and empty.

The plaz door of the third was locked.

Jennifer stooped, taking out a small lockpick. "I can open this," she volunteered.

"Where'd you acquire that gadget?"

"Oh, it was lying around at Molly Briggs's villa. Still has the price tag on it." She straightened up. "There, it's open."

Standing to the side of the doorway, Jolson booted the door open.

After waiting ten seconds, he took a look.

"Ben," said Molly.

She was sitting on the edge of a plazcot. Her eyes were underscored with shadows, and there were several ugly blue welts splotching her bare arms.

Very carefully Jolson helped her to her feet. "Molly Briggs, Jennifer Lenz," he said.

"Pleased to meet you," murmured Molly, letting her head rest against Jolson's chest.

"You okay?"

"As well as can be expected."

"Okay, so we'll take our leave and—"

"She's got Larchmont locked up down here somewhere, Ben. As well as Sally and Lou Killdozer."

Jolson said, "I'd be content to let them fend for themselves, considering the—"

"No, we have to rescue the lot of them," insisted Molly. "You don't want Dr. Windom deciding to—"

"The good doctor is defunct."

"Oh?" Molly stepped back from him. "Even so, it's our duty as accredited operatives to—"

"Detectives don't have a code like robots. We can—"

"No, Ben."

"Okay, okay." He shrugged. "But be assured I'm doing this grudgingly."

They located Joshua Larchmont next. The bewhiskered PlazHartz executive had been locked in the storeroom next to Molly's.

"Had a g-g-good deal of time to do some thinking while I've been held p-p-prisoner here," he informed Jolson as he helped him out of his cell. "Done a b-b-bit of facing the old facts and s-s-searching the soul, as it were. D-d-decided I've been a b-b-bloody fool. Regret it all."

"Good, we can use you to testify against Dr. Windom."

"Ah, don't know if I'd care to g-g-go that far, old man."

"She's dead."

Larchmont straightened up. "In that c-c-case you can c-c-count on me."

Jolson took the lead and they went prowling deeper into the basement.

From behind a yellow door a dedicated thumping was coming.

"Hey, you bums! Let us out of here!"

"That's Lou," said Molly.

"C'mon, c'mon," the private detective was bellowing.

"My poor dear mother is feeling poorly and craves some fresh air."

Jolson nodded to Jennifer.

She picked the lock and opened the door.

Lou Killdozer had shed his blond disguise and looked just about as Jolson had while he was impersonating him. Except that Lou had quite a few lumps and welts on his face.

Sally was sitting on one of the cots, hands folded.

"Hell, it's about time you crumbs pay some attention." He came striding out into the corridor. "I been bopping on that damn door since— Hey, what gives, angel cake?" He'd recognized Molly and was glowering at her.

"We're springing you," answered Jolson. "Let's move."

"Who are you, pretty boy?"

Sally left the cot, came shuffling to the doorway. "Lou. He's got to be the Jolson bozo. Don't go starting any—"

"And why the hell not?" Lou stomped close to Jolson. "If you and this carrot-topped quiff hadn't futzed up my caper, me and Ma wouldn't have had to cool our tokes in this frapping dungeon while—"

"Lou, we can discuss all this later," suggested Molly. "Right now, though, we want to get the heck out of—"

"I'll tell you something else, sweetheart. I ain't all that happy that you and your old man own Daredevils, Ltd. now," he said, taking out a vile cigar and lighting it. "Once I get squared away, you can bet your boody I am going to see my mouthpiece about dissolving the—"

"I've already done the preliminary work on that," Molly told him. "Within a week you and Sally'll be on your own again."

"Oh, yeah? You got some nerve, sneaking around behind my back and that of my dear old ma while—"

"The thing is, Lou, you simply aren't an honorable man."

"Wait now, honey." Sally stepped into the hall. "Don't you go calling my boy names or—"

"You folks have to come along now," cut in Jolson.

"Don't go giving me and the old lady orders, you—"
Zzzzzzzummmmmm!

The beam of Jolson's stungun hit Lou square in his broad chest. He flapped his arms once, hopped and slumped against the wall.

Taking hold of the stunned detective, Jolson tossed him over his shoulder. "We'll leave now."

Sally said, "That wasn't fair."

"You're absolutely right," he agreed, starting for a ramp.

CHAPTER 28

Five small catkids in two-piece sea-green school suits were huddled together beside an immense mound of luggage piled on the sudomarble floor of lobby 6 of the spaceport. Three were crying, one was wailing and the fifth, a plump catboy desperately holding high a sign reading CAMP HELLQUAD ANNUAL SPACE OUTING, was on the brink of doing both.

Jolson, a single suitcase swinging in his right hand, stopped beside the unhappy group. "Having a problem?"

The boy with the sign said, "We've lost the others— fourteen of them—and Mr. Kuddyback."

Jolson scanned the immense glitterwalled room. There were roughly two hundred people—departing passengers, arriving passengers, well-wishers, a few derelicts—moving in random zigzag patterns through the place.

"Would," he asked, "Kuddyback be a hefty owlman in a polka-dot funsuit?"

"That's him," three of them exclaimed, "that's him!"

"He's over by the faxmag stand." Jolson pointed.

The catboy spotted his counselor. "That was a very good piece of detective work, sir."

"It was," agreed Jolson. "Although the fact he has a

sash saying *Camp Hellquad* draped across his chest gave me an important and useful clue." Grinning, he continued on toward the departure gate where he was supposed to meet Molly.

"So you do have a tender side." Jennifer caught up with him, taking his arm.

"I didn't know anybody was watching."

She said, "I came down to see you off, and then I got to worrying that you might be in disguise and—"

"I only do that when I'm on a case."

The young woman was wearing a pale green two-piece sinsilk skirtsuit. Her hair was pulled pack and held with a twist of green ribbon. "Things have been going very well since I saw you last week."

"I hear you're in charge of PlazHartz."

She laughed. "I was just about the only choice the survivors had," she said. "I'm still a major stockholder. Heather Windom never got around to having it taken away from me." She spread her hands wide. "I'll be trying to run things, with the help of some of the loyal people who didn't know what Heather was up to. Or so they say —there I go, sounding cynical."

"That's the best way to approach the PlazHartz organization." They reached his gate, but it wasn't yet open.

"Nothing very sinister can happen there for a while, Ben. The place is awash with government agents, local police and so forth," Jennifer said. "All working at putting a complete stop to the mind-control business."

"You found Dr. Windom's list of everyone who has one of those special hearts?"

"Turns out Mr. Larchmont remembered he knew how to fish one out of her private computer." She sat on a candy-stripe plazbench. "It's going to be a long, complex piece of work—repairing all those hearts with the mind-control addition."

"Mending hearts can be slow work."

Jennifer smiled and said, "One of the things that make me hopeful is that your Briggs Interplanetary Detective Service is going to take over the security for our plant."

"Hmm?"

"It's a shame you have prior commitments back home on Barnum, but I know Molly's highly efficient and she can—"

"What exactly has she promised you?"

Jennifer looked a touch puzzled. "Molly is going to be staying here on Farpa for another few weeks, until she recruits a local staff and has some key people spacejumped in from the Barnum System," she told him. "Her father may even come out if his schedule permits. Ben, didn't you know about any of this?"

"Molly failed to mention it when we had dinner last night," he said. "Fact is, I thought she was joining me here for the jaunt home."

"That was her original plan, I think, but then late last evening she pixed me to say she'd decided to stay and get the whole thing rolling right away," Jennifer said. "Which means a lonesome voyage home for you. I'm glad, though, she's staying to help us out."

"Just so she doesn't recruit Lou Killdozer."

Smiling, she said, "Lou and his mother have already called on me at my new office—did I mention it's in a tower with a very impressive view? They offered us the services of Daredevils, Ltd., and he claimed that he masterminded most of my rescue and just about everything else you and Molly accomplished. I turned them down."

"Hyperspace flight twenty-three for Barnum, Murdstone and Esmeralda now boarding at gate thirteen," spoke a voxbox beneath the bench.

Jolson stood. "Good luck in your business career."

"I'm hoping I don't turn into someone like Heather." She rose, facing him. "That's why my brother Brian hasn't yet made up his mind to join me. He's afraid the whole business is corrupting."

"For him maybe, but you ought to fare well."

She slipped her arms around him, kissed him on the cheek. "We'll meet again."

"Almost certainly." He turned away and took a few steps toward the gate.

"Ar, I almost missed you." Dr. IQ came running up, with a large neowicker basket hugged to him. "Trust I'm not bursting in on anything, Ben."

"Not at all, Doc."

With mittened hands the ratman pushed the basket to him. "I brought you a going-away present."

"I'll wager it's cheese."

"It is," admitted Dr. IQ.

The girl with the rainbow hair made a weary sound. "A fate worse than death," she said in Jolson's direction.

He was seated two stools away at the long licorice-hued plaz bar in the alternate first-class passengers' lounge. Beyond the four-armed green bartender and the floating shelves of glazbottles and plazflasks the seethru wall provided a view of the vast darkness of space.

"What's your latest problem?" he asked her.

Timmy brought over her drink, a deep purple concoction that was murmuring and fizzing, and sat next to him. "What do you mean, *latest?*"

"Last time we met you were about to face a similar fate."

She eyed him. "Shoot, you're that older but still attractive dunk I met en route to the flying playhouse." She dragged her glopurse over from where it'd been resting on the bar. "Should've recognized you right off. Have I ever introduced myself?" From her purse she took the talking business card and handed it to him.

"Yes, Timmy." He dropped it on the bar top.

"INTRODUCING MISS TIMMY TEMPEST, RE-PORTER AT LARGE FOR *GALACTIC VARIETY!*"

"I'm Ben Jolson."

She opened her purse, held it just below the edge of the bar and sidehanded the card into the purse before it could bellow a second time. "They've stuck me with another wretched assignment," Timmy confided. "I'm bound for a smutz of a planet named Murdstone to cover something called the Murdstone Jazz Festival. Nertz."

Jolson took a sip of his mineral water. "What else did you do on Farpa?"

Timmy answered, "Hey, that turned out to be really something. I got attacked by rebels, and then some old coot named Bud Spooner—except that it wasn't him but just a facsimile—used a stunner on me. When I awakened I was in the middle of some dippy military intrigue with just about half the nurfs at this war college suspecting I was a rebel or a spy myself. Our assistant regional editor —a very frowsy toadman named Marcus—had to skycar out from the capital and explain I wasn't. Before I even halfway recover from that wretched mess I have to suffer through a jazz fest—"

"Ben Jolson," squawked all six of the voxboxes floating

up near the curved lounge ceiling. "Passenger Ben Jolson. You have an important telepix call. Please take it in your cabin at once."

Patting Timmy's nearest elbow, he left the stool. "If I don't see you again, Miss Tempest, allow me to give you my heartfelt good wishes."

"Well, thanks," she said, "I guess."

The small oval screen in the buff wall of his small cabin had the image of a medium-sized, middle-aged black man in a three-piece unisuit on it. "Passenger Jolson?"

"The same."

"We have a call coming in to you from Farpa."

"Okay." He dragged a slingchair closer to the screen, straddling it.

"Be advised that we'll be making our hyperspace cross-over in exactly four and one half minutes. At which time all communications with the Hellquad planets—that includes Fumaza, Fazenda and Ferridor as well as Farpa—will, of course, cease. Therefore, we advise—"

"Okay, I'll take the call."

"I am merely trying to—"

"And I appreciate it."

"Very well."

The screen snapped to black. Then dozens of jagged lines of glittering yellow and red dashed across it. Next Molly was there, sitting in the living room of her rented villa.

"Do you know what a call like this costs? Six hundred eighty-four trudollars for the first minute and then eight hundred twenty-six for the second. You'd think it would get cheaper rather than—"

"We don't have that much time."

"Not at these prices."

"The spaceliner's nearly at crossover point, so if—"

"The reason I'm calling," the red-haired young woman told him. "Well, I feel darn bad about not letting you know I wasn't going home on that flight with you. A faxgram delivered to you in your cabin just isn't the same as—"

"Jennifer and Dr. IQ saw me off, so I wasn't completely heartbroken."

"She's very fond of you. In fact, she came close to insisting I keep you on here for a prolonged period to help set up the BIDS agency branch on Farpa," said Molly. "I knew, though, you were eager to get back to your ceramics business."

"That was thoughtful of you."

"Are you fond of her?"

"I'm fond of most all rich heiresses."

"Anyway, Ben, I'm hoping to be back on Barnum in a month or so," continued Molly. "I don't know how you feel, but I thought we worked well together."

"We did."

"In fact, we were closer on this assignment than we've ever been. I'd like to see that continue."

"Let's have lunch when you return and talk it over."

"No, seriously, Ben." Molly gave him an exasperated frown. "I'll tell you something I wasn't intending to. When I was locked in that darn basement by Dr. Windom—and it really seemed like I might die—well, I started thinking about you and what it'd be like if I never saw you again. For a while there I almost convinced myself that I—"

She was all at once gone from the phone screen. The spaceliner had left the Hellquad System.

Jolson watched the dead screen for several seconds. He stood up, shrugged, and then grinned.